DEATH

CURATED

The Possumwood Mysteries Book 7

HOLLY DEY

ISBN: 978-1-959008-00-2

Acknowledgements

I couldn't do this without the love and support of my wonderful family. I love you so much!

Chapter 1

"I'VE LOST HOPE." PC Donovan sighed and wiped the sweat from her forehead.

"Me, too." Her sister, Daisy Engleman, looked at their brother, Rocky. He wasn't paying attention to his siblings. He was busy scanning the Fourth of July crowd. The holiday fell on a Friday, and the burgeoning crowd was kicking off the three-day weekend enthusiastically.

Drew Berlusconi shook his head. "You two are being awfully dramatic, or should I just say, you're Hopeless?" Daisy opened her mouth to speak, but he pointed to a booth selling stained-glass. "She's right over there."

Rocky smiled, and PC followed his gaze. His daughter looked just like her mother, tall and willowy, with wavy chestnut hair that fell to her waist. The detective was glad to see Hope laughing with the stained-glass artisan.

Her niece appeared to be recovering from finding her groom in the supply closet with her matron of honor minutes before the wedding. No longer having a reason to go on her planned month-long honeymoon to Europe, she'd come to Possumwood, hoping to connect with the father she hardly knew.

Daisy adjusted her purse strap. "I'm goin' over to the Biersal tent for one of them persimmon ales. Any of y'all want anything?"

PC raised a fresh *Red, White, and Blueberry!* snow cone. "I'm good."

"What about you, Mama?"

"If they have any iced tea, I'll take some of that. Otherwise, I guess I'll have some water." Rose Donovan nodded to her younger daughter. "You sure you don't need any help, Daisy?"

PC ran her eyes over her mother, looking for signs of fatigue. Rose was recovering well from the hip replacement surgery she had back in January. She was moving almost as fast now as she had been before her fall.

"I'll take an IPA," Drew said as he fished some bills from his pocket.

Terry Gillespie, Rose's boyfriend, handed Daisy some money and said, "Water for me, too, please."

Rose's brow wrinkled. "Rocky, why don't you go with her? After Imogene got mugged last week in the parkin' lot of Marberger's of all places, I'd feel better if Daisy didn't go by herself. Besides, you can help her carry stuff."

PC studied her brother's face. He was a recovering alcoholic and trying so hard to get his life together. He was going to night school to become a certified nursing assistant and attending twelve-step meetings on Tuesday nights. His eyes gave no hint of struggle. And that was good.

"Getting pretty dark. The fireworks'll be starting soon." PC bit off some of the patriotic snow cone. "Do you think that'll bother the bats?"

Drew shook his head. "They left a while ago. Didn't the *Wings Over Possumwood* bat tour guy say they fly out to the cornfields? They won't be anywhere near here."

The detective nodded. "That's right. I remember he said they smell like tortillas because they eat corn moths."

"It'll probably be another hour, hour and a half before the fireworks start. It's only 8:30. But you can't miss the start of it, because they'll have that brass band playing *Stars and Stripes Forever* before it gets going." Drew shifted his weight a little closer to PC. "Did you bring mosquito spray?"

The detective patted her bag.

"Good, 'cuz they're already coming out." Terry slapped Rose's arm. "Just like the criminals. Imogene got mugged, the pharmacy got robbed. We're having a crime wave." Terry pursed his lips and shook his head.

"It always goes up in the summer but seems to be worse everywhere right now." PC handed over the spray can. "I was so busy looking at the quilts that I didn't get to see Lin's painting." She turned to Drew. "What was the theme again?"

"Infinity." He took her elbow. "We'll be back shortly."

Tables with pop-up awnings and white tents marked the perimeter of the downtown Possumwood city park. Drew's tent was about fifty yards to their left, near Main Street. The cream of the entry crop from *The Best Little Art Gallery in Texas'* Fourth of July art contest was housed in a tent equipped with a portable air conditioner.

Drew's assistant, Wilma Gatewood, looked cool, calm, and collected, and PC got an acute case of chill envy. The retired homicide detective ran a hand through her short hair, wondering how bad it was matted with sweat and sunscreen. *Probably sticking up like a haystack in a hurricane.*

"How are we doing?" Drew asked Wilma.

"Pretty good. All the contest exhibitors but one have sold, so we'll be busy getting those ready to ship out over the weekend. You got packing tape and boxes, right?"

"Yes, Wilma."

Wilma waved to the detective. "You coming to the workshop tomorrow, PC? We'll be working on impasto techniques."

"Of course! Wouldn't miss it." PC had attended almost every Saturday afternoon painting workshop Drew's gallery had offered over the six months she'd been in Possumwood.

"Great! See you then."

The detective toured the tent. There were only fifteen pieces, so it didn't take long. A big blue ribbon hung from Lin Youn's painting. She'd done a still life that included a vase of roses, some at the height of their bloom, while others were shriveled and brown. A handful of bright orange rose hips lay scattered on the crisp white tablecloth.

On a separate table, an obsidian sphere, etched and painted with galaxies and nebulae, spun underneath the flow of a table-top fountain, and the piece boasted a third-place ribbon.

She didn't get a chance to find the second-place piece. A crash—as of something hitting hollow metal—startled her, and she rushed to the front of the tent.

"I said I'm not interested!" A young lady in a hot pink tank top glared at a bear of a man.

Drew and Wilma were already standing in the tent opening. People had stopped to stare. PC eyed the dented garbage can lying on its side, turkey leg remnants and snow cone wrappers spilling onto the parched ground.

"Bah!" The man spat on the grass. PC sized him up as at least six foot six, perhaps taller. Thick, dark fur escaped from the neck of his tee-shirt, front and back, and ran down his bulging arms. There was probably more hair poking out of his clothes than sprouting from his balding head. "I will find woman who is pretty!" He stormed off, kicking the trash can again for good measure.

That accent—is he Russian? "Are you all right? What happened?" PC put a hand on the woman in pink's back. She was still shaking. Three other young women crowded around her.

"He asked if I wanted to go party with him and I told him no. Then he started arguing with me about it."

"He's probably off to bother someone else, but it couldn't hurt to ask one of the security officers to walk you to your car when you get ready to leave."

The woman closed her eyes for a moment and nodded. "Good idea."

PC watched her and her friends walk away and blend into the crowd. She turned to Drew. "Who was that guy?"

"Not sure what his name is. I'm sure you've passed by it, but there's a Museum of Slovenian Culture on Main Street, not too far down from Marberger's grocery store. It was built as a boarding house in the 1920s, two story dark red brick with white trim."

"I know exactly where that is. Hope's been volunteering there—she was an exhibit designer at the Burke Museum in Seattle. There doesn't seem to be a lot to the place. I mean, their gift shop only has fridge magnets, hatpins, and some tee-shirts. This guy works there?"

"Two sisters, Jagoda and Cvetka, moved here from Slovenia. It's been ten, fifteen years now. They started the museum, and he came a few years later. He's their younger brother. Not sure what he does there."

"Seems a very niche place, for such a small town."

"Well, there was a tiny Slovenian enclave in Mirabella County. Not sure how many people are left. I doubt the museum takes in much in ticket sales, but they have event space on the second floor—they keep it pretty busy with receptions, banquets, that sort of thing. I think that's probably where they get most of their income. The majority of their exhibits are donated. There are a lot of people of Slovenian descent who like to paint pictures or take photos of their Ljubljana vacations and send them here. I've helped Melanie with the appraisals for their insurance."

PC felt a twinge of jealousy. She'd met the very attractive head curator a few times when she'd dropped Hope off or picked her up. "She seems nice enough."

The first notes of a Sousa march blasted through the sticky evening air. The brass band had set up in the ornate gazebo in the center of the city park that lay between the Mirabella County Courthouse and Possumwood City Hall.

Drew proffered his arm. "I guess the fireworks are about to start."

PC looped her arm through his. "Let's find Mama then."

The Museum of Slovenian Culture opened early on a Saturday morning. Rocky had dropped Hope off on his way to work. PC had just finished feeding Rose's rescued farm animals: Hazel, the three-legged goat, Guinevere and Arthur, the opinionated donkeys, and a small flock of assorted chickens, when her phone rang.

"Aunt Primrose!"

"Hope? What's wrong?"

"You have to get here quick! She's dead!"

Chapter 2

"WHAT?" PC PLUGGED her free ear. "Did you say someone is dead?"

"Yes! Melanie, the curator."

"Okay, okay. Hope, have you called 9-1-1?"

"Cvetka did. Please come, Aunt PC. I'm in trouble."

The call disconnected, and PC swore under her breath as she sprinted for the house. "Come on, Cordite! Hurry, hurry!"

The sandy-colored terrier mix looked up from the piece of donkey hoof trimming he was investigating, saw PC running, and bolted after her.

"Primrose? You get into some wasps?" Rose asked, as her daughter rushed past her in the kitchen.

"No, Mama. Got a call from Hope. She's not hurt, don't worry. But she needs me. Be back soon." The detective scooped up her keys and bag on the way out the front door.

PC arrived in record time. She may have pushed the speed limit a little bit, but she was fairly sure most of the on-duty officers in Possumwood would be at the Museum of Slovenian Culture. Sure enough, red and blue lights bounced off every surface from the four patrol cars parked hastily in the lot. There was also a semi with *Meadowlark Movers* painted on the side of the trailer. The detective hurried to the front door.

"Hey, PC." The female officer blocking the entrance smiled.

"Sanchez. What's going on?"

"The ladies who run the place, Cvetka and Jagoda, heard a noise in one of the galleries just after they'd opened up. No visitors yet. Anyway, they walked into the room and found the curator, Melanie Novak, on the floor, and their volunteer standing over her with a bloody sword in her hand, and blood all over her clothes."

"I see." *Yes, Hope. You are the mushrooms in a whole goulash of trouble.*

"Tran's inside. You can go on in if you want." Sanchez stepped away from the door.

"Thanks."

A clump of men stood near a doorway at the end of the main hall. Crime scene tape stretched across the entryway. The detective took a deep breath and strode down the inlaid marble floor to the group. She was acquainted with most of them, and they barely looked up as she approached. She nodded congenially and ducked under the yellow tape.

The first thing she saw was the body on the floor. Melanie lay with her back to the door, and from here, it appeared she was just resting. PC could smell the salty, coppery scent of blood, though.

"Well, well, well. If it isn't the harbinger of death." The voice of Possumwood Police Chief Elwood Wilson came from her left. "I guess the apple doesn't fall far from the tree."

"What is that supposed to mean, Woody?" PC snapped.

"Your brother hasn't always been… an upstanding citizen."

"Are you talking about the time you falsely accused him of murder, and I had to catch the actual killer for you?" PC's hands shook as she fought to keep her voice from breaking.

"Ouch."

"Where is Hope?"

"You're not even going to ask what happened?" Woody's lip curled into a lop-sided smirk, and it was all PC could do not to slap him. He'd done the same thing when they'd dated almost forty years ago in high school. She'd hated it then, too.

"Fine." PC clenched her jaw. "What. Happened?" *Would his story differ from what Sanchez told me at the door?*

"Since you asked so nicely—"

A gurney clattered on the threshold as two mortuary assistants wrestled it through the single-width back door.

"Dr. Mack!" The chief waved to Dr. McKenzie Chapman, the retired pathologist who was contracted as the Medical Examiner for Mirabella and the three surrounding counties.

"Chief!" He waved back. As he got closer, he regarded the angry detective. "Hey, PC."

"Dr. Mack."

Woody cleared his throat. "As I was going to tell Detective Donovan here, the owners of the museum, Jagoda and Cvetka, had opened the doors at 8:30 to let their employees and one volunteer inside."

The ME rubbed his head. "Don't they open at nine?"

"They weren't ready for business yet. The owners went to the back office while everyone else was getting set up for the day. At

10

approximately 8:45, they heard a crash and investigated. They reported grunting and scuffling coming from this gallery, so they and their front desk employees entered the room. The head curator, Melanie Novak, lay on the floor. Standing over her was the museum's volunteer, Hope Gladstone, holding a sword. She also had a large amount of blood on her clothes. When we searched her, there was an emerald and sapphire peacock brooch in her pocket. We believe Ms. Novak caught her stealing the brooch, and Ms. Gladstone grabbed a sword from the display case and stabbed her."

PC pushed back. "What did Hope say happened?"

"She denied it, of course. She claims she heard the crash, came to investigate, and found Ms. Novak leaning on one of the display cases, sword in her hand. Gladstone took the sword, and tried to catch Novak as she fell, getting the blood on her clothes. Ms. Novak had just hit the floor when everyone else came in."

"And why couldn't it have happened that way?" PC growled.

"The brooch is plenty suspicious. But she also had Cvetka Golob's credit card on her."

"What did Ms. Golob say about it?"

"I haven't spoken with her yet. She's getting the contact information for Miss Novak's family. She'll be out in a minute, I'm sure."

An officer PC didn't really know ducked under the crime scene tape and headed toward them. "Excuse me, Chief. Don't mean to interrupt, but I've got a Darrell Leidecker out in the main gallery that wants to talk to you. He's a freight transporter and says he needs to pick up some crates."

"Okay." He followed the officer out of the small gallery.

PC moved so that she could see and hear the truck driver. Officer Somebody beckoned to a man in a sleeveless plaid shirt, who approached the chief and introduced himself as Darrell Leidecker.

Woody turned to the trucker. "And what is it you are moving for the museum?"

Leidecker handed the chief a clipboard. "Two wooden crates, looks like paintings and a couple of small sculptures. Kind of stuff I usually get from them."

"How often to you get freight here?"

The trucker shrugged. "I probably pick up or drop something off once a week. On average, anyway."

The chief examined the freight invoice. "I'm really sorry, Mr. Leidecker. I can't let you take anything right now. We're investigating a pretty serious crime. Hard to say when your crates'll be available."

Leidecker glanced at the crime scene tape. "My boss told me it was an express delivery—the folks expectin' these are in a hurry to get them. I came early, so I'd be here before the museum opened."

"Did you? What time was that?"

"8:40. I really need to get those crates."

"I can't really help—"

"Who has tracked this water onto my floors?" A scowling woman, likely in her early to mid-sixties, stopped near the driver. Trim and severe, she reminded the detective of Cinderella's wicked stepmother in the original Disney cartoon.

"I'm sorry, Miz Golob. There was a big puddle at the edge of the driveway where I parked my truck."

"Darrell, I am disappointed."

"I'll be happy to mop it up, ma'am."

PC tilted her head and squinted, finally seeing traces of wet footprints. Then again, wet polished marble floors are slicker than a greased polecat, and she didn't want to slip.

Jagoda Golob waved her hand dismissively. "No. Karina will do it."

"Ma'am, the chief here says I can't pick up my load."

Jagoda pursed her lips as her head bobbled at the end of her neck. "There is no load. Melanie was to pack crates this morning. She came early; still, crates are empty. Now, no more Melanie."

Leidecker's mouth opened, then snapped shut. "I'm sorry to hear that, ma'am. I'm sure if you gave her another chance…"

"Bah! Melanie is *mrtev*." She drew her finger across her throat in a slicing motion.

"What…?"

Woody cleared his throat. "Ms. Novak was murdered this morning."

The trucker's jaw worked up and down, like a fish trying to breathe air. "I… I… I'm so sorry, Miz Golob. I don't know what to say."

"Gorman!" the chief called. "Get over here. I need you to take a statement." PC stepped forward, but he shook his head. "Not you."

He was right, of course. It would be an extreme conflict of interest for her to work on her niece's case. But she didn't entirely trust the investigation skills of the Possumwood PD, either, even though they had gotten a lot more practice since January. It seemed like murder dogged her steps like a Hellhound. PC wanted nothing more than to snap a leash on that bad puppy and bring it to heel.

While she watched Dr. Mack finishing up his data gathering, PC eavesdropped on Leidecker's description of what he'd done that morning. He said he arrived at about 8:40 and finished up some paperwork in his truck. By the time he was done, the police were arriving. After seeing officers come and go, and no gunfire had erupted, the trucker came inside to check on the crates.

The funeral home men carefully zipped Melanie's body into a cadaver pouch and lifted her onto the stretcher. Dr. Mack followed them, pausing near Woody to say he'd have the preliminary autopsy report this afternoon.

PC had gotten a better grip on her anger. "Where is Hope?"

"Down at the station, being booked for second degree homicide and possibly two counts of grand larceny."

Tran must have taken her out the front door.

PC nodded, turned on her heel, and strode out the back door of the museum. On the way to her car, she called her Uncle Raymond, the only lawyer she knew in Possumwood. She told him what happened, and he agreed to meet her at the station.

She arrived first. PC doubted Tran would let her talk to Hope, but he might at least tell her something.

Annie Youn, the daughter of Rose's next-door neighbors, and Tran's fiancée, sat at the front desk. "Oh… hey, PC."

"Annie, I really need to talk to Tran. Can you buzz me in?"

"Let me check." She sent a text message.

A moment later, she looked up. "He says it's okay."

"Thanks." PC hurried through the security door.

The keys of Tran's laptop clattered as he sat in his cubicle and typed. He stopped and turned around at her approach.

"I'd like to see my niece."

"Not yet."

"Her lawyer's on the way."

"Good. She's going to need all the help she can get."

"Why is that?"

Tran fidgeted with a pen. "How well do you know your niece?"

"Not that well, actually." PC sucked her teeth, then pulled up a chair from the neighboring cube. "When my brother was 17, he got his girlfriend pregnant. He wanted to marry her, but her mother sent Darla off to live with her grandparents in California. Rocky was already struggling with our father's murder—that hit him so hard, and this just broke him. He dropped out of school after that. Darla, on the other hand, graduated and attended Stanford. Ended up with a fancy tech job in Seattle."

"Did Rocky ever try to go see her and the kid?"

PC sighed. "I think he wanted to. But he was too busy fighting his own demons, and they were winning. He wasn't really in a place where he could even offer child support, much less be a father. Darla got married, but she and Hope's stepdad split up after a few years. He remarried and had kids with his new wife. Darla came to town when her mama passed, and again when her sister got married, so we saw Hope a few times when she was little."

"But you didn't really keep in contact."

"Mama did. She wrote to Darla and Hope from time to time, always sent Christmas and birthday cards. I guess that's how they heard Rocky'd cleaned up his act, and they asked him to walk Hope down the aisle at her wedding."

Tran tapped his pen on his leg. "You know, I can't really talk to you about the case."

PC nodded.

"I'm going to get some coffee. You want any?"

"Sure. Cream, no sugar."

"It may take me a few minutes, but I won't be long."

"Okay."

When Tran got up, PC noticed he hadn't locked his screen, and she could see the document he'd been looking at. It was from the Seattle Police Department.

Hope had a rap sheet.

Chapter 3

PC GLANCED OVER her shoulder to make sure no one was coming, then moved into Tran's chair to get a better look at his laptop. Hope had been arrested six times in Seattle. Three for disorderly conduct, two for trespassing, and one for assault with a deadly weapon. The incidents were sprinkled over the last three years, with the assault being the earliest. All six charges had been dropped.

Someone coughed in the hallway, and she slipped back into her seat.

PC exhaled, grateful it was Tran stepping through the doorway, and not Woody.

"Cream, no sugar." He handed one of the two cups of coffee over to her.

"Thanks."

PC's phone buzzed. "Just pulled up," her Uncle Raymond texted. She rose. "Hope's lawyer's here."

Tran nodded, and the detective threaded her way down the corridor toward the security door. PC met her uncle and another man being escorted by Officer Gorman.

"Primrose!" Uncle Raymond pulled her into a bear hug. When he released her, she took a step back. "This is Michael Barnsdale. He's the best criminal defense lawyer in the county."

Barnsdale was about 6'2" and built like a brick house. His tailored suit accented his broad shoulders and narrow waist, and his teeth were whiter than the South Pole in winter. Charisma billowed off him in waves.

He reached out to shake PC's hand. "It's a pleasure to meet you, Ms. Donovan."

"Likewise. Thank you for coming out to speak with Hope." PC gave him a tense smile.

Gorman cleared his throat. "This way, please."

"Primrose?" Uncle Raymond clasped her shoulder. "Why don't you go on home, and I'll meet you there later?"

PC's hackles rose at being patted on the head and told to run along, but she also knew Rose must be beside herself with worry. "Both of you coming by later?"

"I definitely will."

PC nodded and left.

It was lunchtime, and after she started the car, she decided to stop and pick up something for her and her mother. If Rose was out of sorts, there was a good chance Terry would be there with her. She'd get a plate for Rocky, too. He only worked half a day on Saturdays and would probably be home by the time she arrived.

When PC pulled into the driveway, Rose's car wasn't there. Her mother didn't drive anymore, so she let Rocky use it to get to work and school. The detective peeked at her FlitBit. 12:43.

Huh. Must have gotten wrapped up in work.

The parking lot of the Possumwood PD was clearly visible from the Brisk Rib, and she hadn't seen the car, so Rocky wasn't there. She felt bad for her brother—it was going to be a nasty shock when he got in. He always left his phone turned off while he was at work, so unless Rose had called Durelle Fennec, his boss at the Azalea Manor nursing home, he wouldn't be aware of what had happened.

PC was a little surprised that Cordite didn't meet her at the door. And then she saw why. Rose sat on the couch, sobbing, the little dog licking her arm.

The detective rushed over, dropped the food on the coffee table, and sat beside her distraught mother. "Mama? What's wrong?"

"I tried to stop him." A ragged breath wracked her body. "He wouldn't listen."

"Tried to stop who, Mama? What's going on?"

"Rocky came home from work." Rose blew her nose on a piece of paper towel. "When he found out what happened, he said he was going to straighten things out at the Slovenian Museum. I told him he'd just stir up more trouble, but he lit out of here like a scalded haint. Terry went after him to try and calm things down."

"Alright. I'll go get him." It wouldn't be the first time she'd had to step in to rescue her brother from his own temper.

PC jogged to her car and peeled out of the driveway. When she turned in at of the Museum of Slovenian Culture, the parking lot was mostly empty. The law enforcement vehicles had left, but the Meadowlark Moving truck was still there. Rose's car slashed across three spaces near the back door, and Terry's car was parked nearby. PC pulled in next to Terry and hurried inside, apprehensive about what she might find.

In the center of the main exhibit hall, the man who had accosted the young lady at the 4th of July festival loomed over Rocky and Terry, who was tugging on Rocky's arm. Darrell, the truck driver, stood between Rocky and the huge man, arms outstretched to keep them apart.

Two older ladies, one of whom was Jagoda, and the other PC assumed to be Cvetka, were having a heated discussion between themselves in what was most likely Slovene. The detective's shoulders slumped when she noticed her brother's lip was bleeding.

Rocky, what have you done?

Only the cashier looked up from behind the counter as PC approached the tight knot of people.

"Now, now. Everybody's all upset, but let's be reasonable here." Darrell's voice was calm as a sleeping cat.

The tall man roared, "His whelp kill our Melanie!"

"That *may* be true, Branislav. But you don't know that, not for sure." Darrell shook his head slowly, knowingly.

"If Hope stabbed her, it was self-defense, pure and simple!" Rocky pointed an accusing finger at Branislav.

"Hey, guys." PC said as cheerfully as she could manage. "What's going on?"

"I call police!" Not-Jagoda brandished her phone.

"Cvetka! No more police!" Her sister snatched the device out of her hand.

While they argued, PC focused on the males. "Rocky? How was your day at work?"

"What? It was fine. Why are you asking me that?"

11

Because you need to calm down before Bran here grinds your bones to make his bread. "So, I'm guessing this means you've heard about Hope."

"Of course, I've heard about Hope! Why do you think I'm here?"

"Why *are* you here?"

"Because… because…" Rocky waved his hands in frustration.

"If you get arrested for assault, you'll get kicked out of your CNA program. How is that going to do Hope any good?"

He sighed deeply and wiped his lip with the back of his hand, smearing blood across his cheek.

PC's sigh was inward. "Why don't you and Terry go back to the house? I picked up lunch, and I'll be right behind you."

"But they—"

"Rocky, nothing you're doing here is going to help Hope. You're just making things worse. What's it going to look like if you get arrested, too?"

Her brother covered his face with his hands, then swiped them down until they met in a prayer position under his jaws. He stood there, chin resting on his fingertips, as seconds dragged by. "You may be right." He started turning toward the door.

Branislav reached past Darrell and sucker punched Rocky in the head. He went down hard on the cold marble.

"Branislav!" Cvetka and Jagoda screeched together.

"For Melanie," he growled as he stormed off up the marble staircase.

PC kneeled beside her brother. His bell had clearly been rung. From the looks of things, it was still ringing. "Rock? Rocky, can you sit up?"

Moving slowly, he got to all fours, then shook his head, trying to clear the cobwebs. Blood from his broken lip glistened on the white tile.

"Karina!" Jagoda shouted.

Moments later, a young woman appeared with a roll of paper towels and some cleaning spray. She handed PC a wad of towels, and the detective held it to her brother's lip.

"You're gonna need stitches for that."

"I can drive you to the clinic—Dr. Chowdry keeps office hours on Saturdays." Terry said.

"That is so kind of you, Terry." PC looked up at her mother's boyfriend. "But you know what would really be helpful? If you go home and stay with Mama. I'll get Rocky patched up. I stopped by the Brisk Rib and got lunch—it's there on the coffee table."

"Great idea. Can I help you get him up?"

"I got it, thanks. Uncle Raymond might be there by the time we get back. You just go take care of Rose."

PC helped Rocky to his feet, and Karina got busy with the cleaning solution before the blood seeped any further into the grout.

"I'm sorry, ladies, for the disturbance," PC said to Cvetka and Jagoda as she started Rocky toward the back door.

Once outside, she unlocked her car. "I need your keys."

"What?"

She gestured to his abysmal parking job. "So I can fix the car. And I'll probably have to come get it later."

He handed them over and sat in PC's SUV while she parked his car properly. She got into her own vehicle and started driving. The Possumwood Family Clinic was located in the Courthouse square, right across the street from Karla's Kurls, the beauty parlor where Daisy worked. *I sure hope she doesn't keep Saturday hours.*

PC waited for traffic to clear on Main Street before she pulled out. "Rocky, I know you're upset. We all are. But picking fights isn't going to solve anything."

"Sorry I lost my cool. But you don't understand. Hope is such a kind, gentle person. She'd never hurt nobody."

A kind, gentle person with six arrests in Seattle. "I understand you're trying to make up for lost time. But I don't think sitting in the cell opposite her in the Possumwood City Jail is going to help that along."

He might have smiled, but PC couldn't tell underneath the bloody paper towel.

"I don't want to believe that she's a killer, either. But the Possumwood PD is not going to talk to me on this one. I need your help."

"*My* help? What is it you think I can do?"

"You can talk to Darla, see what's been going on in Hope's life. They'll let *you* visit her. They may not let me. I can give you questions to ask."

Rocky grunted as PC hit a bump. "You make it sound like Uncle Raymond won't be able to bail her out."

"I guess we'll find out at the arraignment on Monday. There's a chance they'll consider her a flight risk and deny bail altogether.

Woody's asking the DA to charge her with second degree murder and grand larceny. If the judge grants bail, it may be so high we can't pay it anyway."

"I have some money saved up."

"A million dollars?"

Rocky bowed his head.

"Uncle Raymond is with her now." PC stopped for a red light. "He got the county's top criminal defense lawyer for her. That's what he said. The best. If she's innocent, he'll get her off."

"*If* she's innocent? What do you mean 'if'?"

"As I said before, I want her to be innocent. Really. I do. But looking at it as a homicide detective, I have to say, it looks pretty open and shut. Hope was holding the murder weapon, standing over the decedent, covered in blood. She also had an expensive brooch and Cvetka's credit card in her pocket."

"Oh? So now you're saying my daughter is a thief?"

PC shook her head. "That's not what I'm saying. She had two valuable items that didn't belong to her on her person. There could be a reasonable explanation, but I don't know what it is. I don't have access to the files, and I haven't been able to talk to her."

"It looked like an open and shut case when Woody thought I killed Heather Michah."

PC exhaled deeply as she pulled into a parking space. "That's different."

"How?"

"You weren't standing over a body with a bloody weapon in your hand, for one thing."

"What's the other thing?"

PC opened her door. "I know you. I knew you didn't do it."

"Hope did not murder that woman."

"Then help me prove it."

Chapter 4

PC SAT IN the waiting room of the Possumwood Family Clinic, waiting on Dr. Chowdry to stitch up her brother's lip and check him for signs of a concussion.

She pulled out the notebook she always carried and jotted down a few notes.

Hope claims Melanie was holding the sword when she entered the room. She tried to catch Melanie when she collapsed, and that's how she came to be covered in the victim's blood.

Where did the brooch come from? Why did Hope have it?

Why did she have Cvetka's credit card?

Is it possible Melanie stabbed herself?

With a sword? Unlikely.

Did anyone else have access to the gallery where she was found?

Yes—it connected with both the main gallery and the adjacent one, as did all the smaller galleries. The museum was a big rectangle with a lengthwise wall partitioning off about a third of the room from the main gallery.

That narrow section was divided crosswise into four smaller galleries. Each of those rooms connected with its neighbor on either side and the main gallery. Someone could theoretically have stabbed Melanie, then run into the next gallery, and the next, and so on until they came out behind the rest of the employees, then slipped into the group unnoticed. Or out the front door. She made a brief sketch.

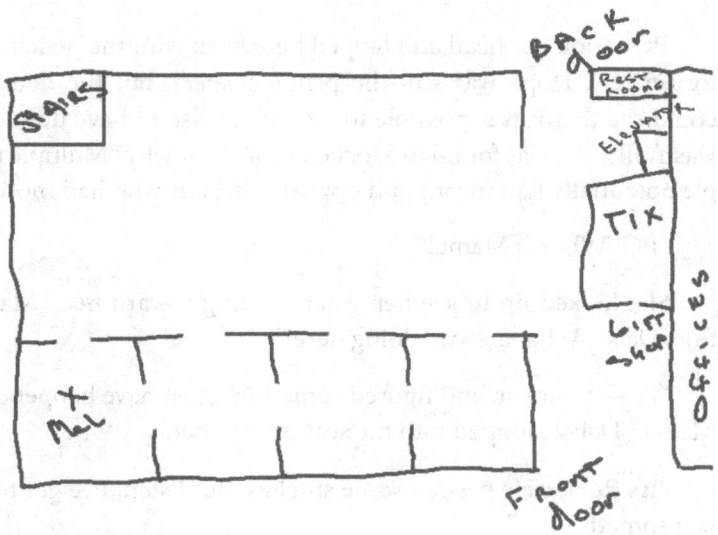

Who would have a reason to kill the curator? Neither of the museum owners seemed upset by her passing, and that was notable.

Branislav was angry, though. *Had he asked her out, then gotten violent when she said no, like he did with the girl on the 4th of July?*

What about the sisters? Did they disapprove of their brother's interest in her and decided to remove the temptation? Or were they angry she didn't bend to his fancy, and things got out of hand when they tried to force her to comply?

Seems it would have been much easier to just fire her. Unless… Melanie knew something she wasn't supposed to, and they didn't want her running her mouth.

PC shook her head and tapped her cheek with the pencil. Unfortunately, Hope was still the prime suspect, but the detective could see that it was possible for someone else to have done it. It wasn't like she was found in a locked room. But why? Multiple people potentially had means and opportunity, but who had motive?

"PC! Where's Mama!"

She looked up to see her sister striding toward her. "Mama's fine, Daisy. What are you doing here?"

"I saw your car, and figured somethin' must have happened to Mama." Daisy plopped into the seat next to her.

"It's Rocky. He needed some stitches. But listen, I've got to tell you something—"

"Why's Rocky need stitches?"

"That's what I'm trying to tell you. I'm glad you're sitting down. Hope's been arrested for murder."

"Murder!"

The receptionist peered over the counter at them.

"Keep it down, Daisy. They found her holding a bloody sword and standing over the dead body of Melanie Novak from the Slovenian Museum."

Daisy's hand flew to her mouth. "Do you think she…?"

"I don't know." PC shrugged. "I don't *want* to think so. As soon as Rocky found out, he got up a big head of steam and went barreling over to the museum to have it out with… who knows? He got into a fight with Branislav Golob."

"Oooh. Bran is a big ole boy. He comes into Karla's Kurls every month on the fifteenth, just like clockwork, for a haircut."

"Huh. I would have pegged him as more of a barber shop kind of guy."

"Well, in cosmetology school, we're taught how to cut hair for both men and women, so it don't really matter. But I think he likes bein' surrounded by all the girls. He's a real good tipper. There's usually a fight over who gets him in her chair."

"Have any of the beauticians dated him?"

Daisy's mouth made a little 'o' as she sucked in a breath. "If Karla ever found out one of her girls was datin' a client, she'd have a hissy fit. I mean, unless they was already goin' out beforehand. That'd be different." She twirled a lock of her bottle-blonde hair around her finger.

"That's not a definitive no."

Daisy studied her manicure.

"Hope looks 99% guilty at this point. If there's a chance, no matter how small, that someone else had reason to kill Melanie, now would be a good time to come out with it."

"I don't wanna get nobody fired."

"If she did it, she's going to lose her job, anyway. If Hope is the only suspect…" PC shrugged.

Daisy closed her eyes and breathed deeply. "Maribel was seeing him. Usually, they'd go somewhere on the weekend so they wouldn't run into anyone they knew."

"Maribel?

"Rodriguez. You probably remember her—she's Jill Franco's little sister."

"I didn't realize her name was Maribel. Jill always called her 'Peanut.' Is she the jealous type?"

"Kinda. But she was in the shop all morning."

"What time does the beauty parlor open on Saturday?"

"9:00."

It would take ten minutes or less to get from the Slovenian Museum to Karla's Kurls, leaving at least five minutes to clean up. "Interesting. What time do you have to clock in?"

"8:30, to get everything set up."

"And when did Maribel show up?"

"She got there five minutes late—she had car trouble, and her sister dropped her off. I remember that, 'cause Jill was real mad about somethin'. I thought she was talkin' about a pagoda, but I'm not sure."

PC shifted her eyes to the door that led back to the exam rooms for a long moment. "Well, there aren't any pagodas in Possumwood."

But there is a Jagoda.

"Have you been to the Slovenian Museum, Daisy?"

Daisy smiled. "When Zachary was in seventh grade, he had a powerful crush on a little gal in his class named Samantha. He was so desperate to impress her that he wanted to take her to the museum so he could show her how classy he was. I drove 'em there, hung around, then we had lunch at the City Café."

Daisy sighed, and a tear sparkled in the corner of her eye. "I cain't believe he's goin' off to play college football next month. Don't know what Tyson and I are gonna do without him."

The detective put her arm around her sister. "It'll be all right."

"I'm gonna miss him so much. And I also worry about him gettin' hurt. He's on a football scholarship..."

"You have to stop worrying. That's not gonna do anybody any good. Things will work out. I'm sure he'll call you on weekends, the ones he doesn't turn up on your doorstep with a bundle of dirty laundry."

Daisy made a noise, and PC couldn't decide if it was a strangled laugh or a choked sob.

The door to the exam rooms finally opened.

"Okay, I'll see you in ten days." Rocky waved to someone in the hall behind him, a slip of paper clutched in his fingers. He turned around, then stopped as if he were stuck in a glue trap. "Daisy? What are you doing here?"

Daisy gave an exasperated sigh. "You know I work across the street, right?"

PC stood up. "What did the doctor say, Rock?"

"Looks like a mild concussion, supposed to just rest for two or three days. Then I get the stitches out a week on Monday. She gave me a prescription." He waved the small piece of paper.

"Glad to hear it.

"The bad thing is, she told me not to drive before Tuesday. How'm I gonna get to work? To class?"

"I think you're going to have to take Monday off."

His eyes stayed on the ground as they walked out to the parking lot.

"Daisy, if I drop you off at the Slovenian Museum, would you drive Mama's car back to her house?"

"Sure. And I can stay for a while. The boys are at their daddy's helpin' him fix fences. Probably be back late this evenin'. Tammyjo don't like them spendin' the night there." Daisy's lips pursed.

"It'll be good to have family around." Rocky's smile was unconvincing.

"I have an appointment at 2:00, so I can drop you back here on my way, Dais." *An appointment with impasto.*

"That'd be great."

PC and Cordite came in from feeding the animals to find Daisy and Rocky cooking dinner under Terry's supervision. Rose sat in the living room, discussing Hope's case with Uncle Raymond. While the detective paused at the kitchen sink to wash her hands, Cordite began to whine and bark at the front door. PC walked through to the living room, where she could see her dog sitting, staring up at the doorknob, his wiry tail thumping on the rug.

Seconds later, the doorbell rang.

PC turned to Rose. "Somebody coming over?" She hoped it was Michael Barnesdale.

Rose shook her head.

The detective opened the door, expecting to see the attorney she'd met earlier. She blinked several times in surprise.

"Hello, Darla."

Chapter 5

THERE WAS NO mistaking Hope's mother. She had that same luxurious chestnut mane, but hers was swept back into a severe French twist that looked travel weary. Dark circles underlined her large aquamarine eyes.

"Come in." PC stepped aside.

"Thank you." Darla rolled her carryon across the threshold, and as soon as she was clear of the door, bent to pet Cordite. "What's your name, cutie patootie?"

The dog rolled onto his back for a tummy rub and Darla delivered the scritchy-scratches.

PC smiled at her dog. "That's the first time I've ever seen Cordite do that for a stranger."

Darla straightened up and set her bag against the wall. She turned toward Raymond. "Thank you for calling me, Mr. Ramos. I appreciate you looking after Hope."

Raymond got to his feet. "She's my great niece. It's not a big ask."

"Oh, Darla, honey…" Rose stood up and gave her a long hug.

When Darla pulled away, she gave Rose a peck on the cheek. "When we were in Dallas, Rocky told me about your accident and your surgery. I wish I'd known sooner, but I'm glad you're doing well."

"I didn't want you to worry."

"You have always been very kind to me."

Movement caught PC's eye, and she saw Rocky, Daisy, and Terry crowding in the kitchen door. "You may as well come in and say hi, instead of gawking at her like she's a zoo exhibit."

PC could practically see little Valentine hearts in Rocky's eyes. She hoped he wouldn't get his heart broken again, but it was nearly inevitable.

Terry extended his hand as he walked into the living room. "I don't believe we've met. I'm Terry Gillespie."

Darla took his hand. "Perhaps not, but I've heard a lot about you from Rose's letters."

Terry blushed.

Rocky and Daisy crowded around Darla. He put his hand on her shoulder. "You must be real tired." He glanced at her bag. "Were you, uh, gonna stay here?"

"No. Sister's house. Laptop's in there. Didn't want to leave it in the car."

PC couldn't tell if he was relieved or disappointed.

Daisy gave a shy wave. "Hey, Darla."

"Hey, Daisy. How are the boys?"

"Good. They're good."

The trickle of conversation ran dry. After a few long moments, Raymond broke the awkward silence. "Sit down, take a load off. The arraignment's at 10:00 tomorrow morning. Do you need a ride?"

"I have a rental."

PC's nose twitched. "What's that smell?"

She stood and peered through the large serving window between the living room and kitchen.

"Oh!" Daisy hurried toward the kitchen. "I forgot to take the biscuits out of the oven!"

Daisy opened the heavy oven door and a thick, pungent vapor billowed out. The combo detector began to scream. She dumped the smoking carbohydrate ruins into the sink and ran water over them. The oven still exhaled sooty breath.

PC rushed to help. "I'll open some windows!"

She slid open the window above the sink, then propped open the door to the back porch and the outside door, leaving the screen door closed.

"Do you have a fan, Mama?" Rocky asked, waving a flattened cereal box he'd plucked from the recycling.

"I think there's a couple in the garage."

Rocky headed out to look for them, and PC did the same for the front porch doors as she had done for the back, making sure to pull the screen tightly closed—the last thing she needed was for Cordite to slip out into the unfenced front yard. "Hopefully, we can get a cross-breeze."

"I found two!" Rocky returned triumphantly, carrying a square fan and a cylindrical one.

Terry grabbed one from him. "I'll plug this one in."

Even with two fans on, white smoke poured from the oven. Raymond slammed the door closed and twisted the knob to off. "Daisy, you dropped two biscuits on the heating element, and they're on fire."

Panic discolored her voice. "What do we do?"

"It's done. They'll burn out in there. You okay?"

Daisy hung her head. "Yeah. I'm so sorry."

"No." Darla came in and hugged her. "I suppose I knocked everyone for a loop when I showed up on the doorstep unannounced. It's my fault."

Rocky leaped to her defense. "Darla, don't be sorry. Hope's your daughter, just as much as she's mine. You have every right to be here."

Cordite howled.

"What's gotten into him?" Rose asked.

PC sighed. "Sirens."

"I don't' hear an—"

Sirens wailed, getting louder by the second.

Someone pounded on the front screen door. "Rose? Rose, are you in there? PC?"

The detective hurried to greet the visitor. "We're okay. Come on in, Lin. Daisy just set some biscuits on fire."

Rose's next-door neighbor stepped into the house. "Oh, thank goodness! I smelled smoke, then saw it coming from your house. I called the fire department. The dispatcher—Annie wasn't working tonight, so don't blame her—wanted me to stay on the line and talk. I finally had enough and came to make sure you got out."

"Oh, Lin. You are such a good neighbor." Rose had tears in her eyes.

Emotion, or smoke?

The wail of the sirens was almost to the house.

"I'll go out and tell them to stand down." PC threaded her way to the front door.

She waited at the end of the driveway for the ladder truck to come to a stop. She waved to the driver, and he rolled his window down.

"We're all okay. Just something burned in the oven."

"Still have to check it out," called the firefighter in the passenger seat. He burst from the door fully dressed out, slipping on his respirator and helmet as he jogged to the house. By the time PC caught up, Daisy was standing in the living room in tears, her cheeks nearly as red as the flaring embers of the biscuits. Everyone else was clustered around the kitchen door, watching the firefighter.

"Daisy, you okay?"

She nodded. "That's Rusty Applewhite, the boys' football coach. I'm so embarrassed, I could just die."

Applewhite's voice blasted from the kitchen, lecturing Rose about the need for a kitchen fire extinguisher.

PC gave her sister a half-hug. "This, too, shall pass."

The volunteer firefighter swaggered out of the kitchen. He nodded to PC with a smirk. "Everything's ok, ma'am. Just keep those fans running for a while."

"Thanks."

Raymond stood in the kitchen doorway and watched him leave. "Well, at this point, we should probably go out for dinner."

"Oh, come to the Lucky Wok—you can have the event room. It's not booked up tonight." Lin spread her arms, her hands palms up.

"Oh, we couldn't impose," Terry said.

"It's no imposition. Please. Come."

Rose threw her arms around her friend. "Of course we will!"

Darla sat between PC and Rocky at the large round table in the party room at the Lucky Wok. "This place wasn't here the last time I was in Possumwood."

"The food's pretty good, and the Youns are great people." PC studied the woman's face. Her skin had the greyish cast of exhaustion.

"Glad to hear it."

PC felt bad about putting Darla through the wringer, but it had to be done, and done before she passed out into her lo mein.

"Darla, I'm sure you're anxious to eat and get to bed, but I need to ask you some questions about Hope."

Darla nodded slowly.

Rocky jumped in. "Can't this wait 'til tomorrow? You can see how tired she is."

"I'm sorry. It can't. It may have some bearing on what her lawyer tells the judge tomorrow."

Raymond, who was on the other side of PC, nodded. Rocky patted Darla's hand.

PC sipped her iced tea. "There's not a good way to approach this, so I'll be blunt. Hope was arrested six times in the last three years. Can you tell me about that, starting with the assault charge?"

"What?" Rocky asked loudly enough that everyone at the table turned to look.

The detective held a finger to her lips to shush him.

Darla sighed. "Hope had been dating this guy. I told her that I got a bad vibe from him, but she didn't care. He did a lot to gaslight and control her. She'd started to see what he was up to and broke it off with him. Right there at the restaurant, he stabbed himself in the abdomen with a steak knife and started screaming that she was trying to kill him. The police arrested Hope for assault. However, he didn't count on there being security cameras on the patio. Charges dropped. And it turned out he'd stolen a credit card offer out of her mail and opened an account in her name. Whole bunch of other stuff turned up—he's in jail now."

"Excellent!" Raymond bit his lip. "About the charges being dropped. Not that she was in an abusive relationship."

Darla gave him a hard look but continued. "Hope belongs to an activist group that organizes marches and protest events. She got arrested twice for chaining herself to an old-growth redwood tree to save the grove from development. The other times, it was for protesting on the governor's lawn after he was reluctant to set Susan Hooper free after DNA evidence proved she wasn't a killer. They saved her from a life sentence in prison with no chance of parole."

Raymond nodded his head. "This is great information. I'm texting Michael with it right now." He pulled out his phone.

"We're doing everything we can, Darla." PC scooped up some bean sprouts.

"I know. Now this lawyer. How good is he? I can get one of the top attorneys in Houston if he isn't the best."

Raymond set his phone on the table. "Michael Barnsdale is the best criminal defense attorney in Mirabella County. He'll do a fantastic job. Just wait and see how he handles the arraignment on Monday."

Darla moved some noodles around her plate. "When I first started working for a tech startup, one of the incentives was stock options. A whole lot of stock options. Money isn't an issue. I'm happy to pay Mr. Barnsdale his regular fee, plus a bonus, for his successful defense of my daughter. But I won't hesitate to bring in some big guns if that seems to be warranted."

"I understand your frustration, Darla. The legal system can be...Byzantine. But just because Michael Barnsdale lives in a small town doesn't mean he isn't an excellent lawyer. He used to work at one of those high-powered firms you keep referring to."

"I'm aware of that." Darla drank some tea. "I looked into him while I was on the plane. The fact that he abruptly quit his partnership at Peterson, Klein, & Barnsdale is what concerns me. What happened?"

Raymond considered the sole remaining broccoli floret on his plate. "His son died of a drug overdose. Then his wife left him— she blamed Michael. Too many hours at the office and not enough being a father." The attorney impaled the floret forcefully, as if punishing it for his friend's tragedy. "He went through some tough times, and... he needed a change of pace."

"Thank you for telling me." Darla pushed her plate away. "I'm exhausted, so I'm going to Rachel's to turn in."

Rose flourished her napkin. "You give your sister a big hug from me."

"I will." Darla reached into her wallet and left a $100 bill on the table. "Sorry, I don't have any change. I'll see you tomorrow." She paused and returned to the table. "Did anyone take Hope her medication?"

Medication?

Nobody responded.

"It's okay. I'll pick it up when I get my things."

"Can I get you something to drink?" Rocky asked hopefully.

Darla yawned. "I would really love a bottle of water."

He went into the kitchen to fetch one from the pantry.

"Let me see if I can find Hope's medication," PC said.

She turned and went into the bathroom that separated her bedroom from Rocky's. PC opened the medicine cabinet and there it was, a prescription for Hope Gladstone.

Aripiprazole.

The detective looked it up on her phone. Treats schizophrenia, bipolar disorder, and depression. PC sighed and headed back to the living room.

Darla said her goodbyes and left. Rocky, Rose, and Terry settled in to watch TV. PC couldn't sit still, however. She took Cordite out for a potty break in the back yard. The critters were munching hay from the manger. Twilight was coming but hadn't arrived yet. The last of the honeysuckle blossoms gave off a perfume that lingered in the hot, damp air. The dog inspected his favorite tree for any news updates.

PC leaned on the wood fence that separated the livestock paddock from the back yard and absently watched the donkeys.

Alright, Jill. What kind of beef are you having with Jagoda? I doubt you're building a pagoda at your Mexican restaurant.

She glanced at her FlitBit.

It's Saturday night. Jillibella's is probably open 'til at least ten. There's plenty of time.

"C'mon Cordie! Let's go inside."

He pretended not to hear her.

"Chicken jerky?"

His head whipped around, and he bounded toward her. They rushed inside, and she paid the bribe before picking up her keys.

"Hey, Mama? I'm going out for a little bit."

Rose leaned forward. "Are you meeting Drew?"

"Not this time."

"When's the last time you two went on a date?"

Breathe in patience. Breathe out annoyance.

"'Bye, Mama."

Jillibella's Mexican Cantina was dangerously near the Possumwood Police Department. She doubted she'd run into any officers, since it wasn't too close to a shift change. She'd keep her eyes open, just in case, though.

PC stood near the hostess stand, surveying the room. The restaurant was a little more than half full, but she didn't spot any of Possumwood's finest.

"What are you doing here? I already talked to the cops once today."

Chapter 6

JILL FRANCO STOOD at the hostess stand, fingers hovering over the menus. PC had gone to school with her from seventh grade on, and they'd gotten along well enough. Not close friends, but not enemies, either. Amicable acquaintances, perhaps. They'd seen each other a few times since PC had returned to Possumwood and were on friendly terms.

Now, PC had to make a decision. Act dumb and play the old friend card, or imply it was an official visit and appeal to authority?

"Can we talk?" PC looked around the busy restaurant. "In private?"

Jill also scanned the dining room. "I can give you five minutes. Hold on." She waved to the kitchen, where the cooks were placing food on a counter to be delivered by waitstaff. "I need Christine."

A few seconds later, a woman who looked only slightly older than PC and Jill came out of the swinging metal doors.

Jill tapped the stand. "I need you to hold down the fort for a few minutes. I won't be long."

Christine replied with a humorless smile.

The restaurant owner led PC to her cramped office, where they each sat down, Jill behind her desk and PC in the guest chair.

"Thanks for taking a minute. You might have heard that my niece, Hope Gladstone, has been arrested for the murder at the Slovenian museum."

Jill leaned back in her chair and covered her chest with her hand, as if she was about to recite the Pledge of Allegiance. "I'd heard it was somebody from out of town, but I hadn't realized she was your niece. Your brother's daughter, right? Daisy doesn't have any girls…"

"Yeah. She's from Seattle. Since you're short on time, let me cut to the chase. Did you have a situation with Jagoda Golob at the museum?"

Jill's eyes narrowed and her lips tightened. "Did I! Ugh! You know how they have events on the second floor? Well, the Mirabella County Jaycees Club had their quarterly meeting there last week. The museum arranged for us to cater it as part of their event package. We've done it plenty of times before, and it's worked fine. This time, though, Jagoda's check bounced."

"I can see why you'd be angry."

"Yeah. I didn't find out about it until yesterday afternoon, so I went first thing this morning to talk to her. I'd already made orders and paid my people based on that money being in my account, and now *my* checks are going to bounce."

"And what time did you get there?"

"Not sure. I dropped Maribel off at the beauty shop a little after 8:30. Then it's what? Five? Ten? minutes to the museum from there?"

"Something like that." *So that puts you there 8:40, 8:45. Right around the time of the murder.* PC wished she had something to drink.

"Anyway, when I got there, the front doors were locked, so I left. I had deliveries coming to the restaurant, and I couldn't hang around indefinitely. Figured I'd try again after lunch."

Jill seemed relaxed, and she was neither avoiding eye contact nor making too much of it. If she was lying, she was very good at it. "Did you notice anything out of place? Any strangers in the area?"

"There was an eighteen-wheeler in the back parking lot, but I didn't get a good look at it. Other than that, there was nothing unusual."

"Did you know Melanie Novak?"

Jill shook her head. "Only by sight. I dealt with Jagoda. If that's all, I need to get back."

"Thanks for taking the time."

Jill led the way to the dining room. PC hadn't planned to stay, but as she rounded the corner, she nearly bumped into Drew Burlesconi. He and a man she didn't recognize were at the hostess stand, waiting to be seated.

Drew grinned. "PC!"

"Hey, Drew." She glanced over at Jill, who retrieved three menus. She was stuck now.

"Booth or table?"

"Booth," Drew answered, then took PC's elbow.

Jill led them to the back of the dining area, where red vinyl-clad benches and tables lined the wall. Drew gestured for PC to slide into the booth first.

"I'm going to the ladies' room. I'll be right back." She didn't really need to go; she just didn't want to be trapped in the booth.

She made her way to the bathroom and washed her hands, then spent a minute or two looking at the black velvet paintings of tango dancers that lined the narrow hallway.

Once she sat down, Drew asked, "Do you know Omar?"

"I'm afraid I don't."

The man across from her wore a stained golf shirt and wrinkled khakis. His downcast eyes had the moist look of suffering. He slowly raised them to meet the detective's. "I'm Omar Schmidt."

"Omar owns the Dollarmore store."

PC nodded. "Yes, I know where that is. Listen, I don't want to intrude…"

Drew's fingers brushed her hand. "You're not intruding. Omar's had some bad news, and I thought he could use a margarita." His eyes widened. "Don't worry. I'm driving, and I'm sober as a judge."

PC gave him a fraction of a smile. If only the drunk who'd crashed into her fiancé all those years ago had had a designated driver.

A server brought a basket of tortilla chips and two small bowls of Jillibella's amazing roasted red pepper salsa, and they ordered drinks. PC and Drew both had water. Omar had the above-top-shelf margarita with two kinds of tequila and a shot of limoncello. There was enough alcohol in there to knock down a bear.

PC didn't want to pry, but she was itching to know what kind of bad news Omar had gotten.

He picked up a chip and traced a design on his plate. "I can't believe it. Everything that's happened. And now she's gone."

PC turned to Drew.

"His girlfriend. She worked at the Museum of Slovenian Culture. Her name was—"

"Melanie." PC finished his sentence.

Drew cocked his head. "How did you know? Of course, your police friend must have told you."

PC nodded. "Mr. Schmidt, I'm very sorry for your loss."

"Thank you." He swirled the liquid in the bottom of his glass. "I shouldn't be this sad about it." Omar buried his face in his hands.

"Why is that?"

Drew raised his eyebrows in PC's direction.

Omar groaned. "I think she was cheating on me with that big oaf that works at the museum. I confronted her about it, but she said I was crazy. And then, I'm embarrassed to say, I screamed at her that we were finished. I don't think I can ever show my face in the Brisk Rib again. Then she called me yesterday. We were supposed to have lunch and see if we could patch things up." Then he swore softly.

"Mr. Schmidt?" PC probed gently.

"I'm sorry. I'm just so angry. And so…" He shrugged. "I didn't want her to die. I was still in love with her. God knows why."

"What happened?"

Schmidt fiddled with his silverware. "The store manager called in sick, so I had to cover her shift. I called Melanie to reschedule our lunch, and—and *he* answered her phone."

"Branislav?"

The store owner nodded.

PC leaned back against the booth. "I'm really sorry. If it helps, Jagoda said Melanie was supposed to come in early to pack crates. Perhaps she couldn't get to her phone."

"Maybe. I just heard his smarmy voice and hung up." He took a gulp of his margarita.

Easy there, hoss. "I know this may seem like a weird question, but what time did you call her?"

Drew elbowed PC in the ribs. She slid away a few inches.

Schmidt blinked like a sleepy owl. "What time?"

PC breathed deeply to keep the edge off her voice. "Yes. What time did you make the call?"

He picked at the salt on the rim of his glass. "Not sure. Probably around 8:30."

PC nodded agreeably. "I see."

That gives you plenty of time to get to the museum to fight with her, and stab her in a jealous rage.

Drew tactfully changed the subject, and PC sat with them through two big bowls of chips and one and a half monster margaritas. She learned way more about the dollar store business than she thought was possible to know. But it kept Omar from getting too maudlin. After a while, they were the only table in the restaurant and the kitchen staff was hanging around the door. Fortunately, Drew had paid their check a while ago.

PC nudged him. "I think we should probably get out of here."

He glanced at his watch. "Oh, wow. You're right. Come on Omar. Let's get you home."

"I don't wanna go, and you can't make me." He crossed his arms and pouted.

Great. A belligerent drunk.

"Omar," Drew coaxed. "Why don't you crash at my house? I've got a wet bar, and we could play some cards or something."

Schmidt's eyelids drooped, and he struggled to keep them open. "Shounds good."

He got to his feet and swayed. Drew put an arm around his back as he stumbled. "I got you."

"Night." PC nodded to the restaurant staff.

Jill waved to her, and she returned the gesture.

The detective watched as Drew helped Omar into the passenger seat of his car. Once he'd closed the door, she said, "You're a good friend."

He opened his mouth to speak, then seemed to think better of it. He patted the hood. "I'd better get him to my house before he passes out."

"Good plan."

"Hey, you know there's a new restaurant opening on Friday, right?"

PC tilted her head. "No. Hadn't heard about it."

"It's called Cajun Spice. You wanna go check it out?"

"Sure."

He grinned. "Great. We'll hash out the details at darts on Wednesday."

PC couldn't help but grin back. "See you then."

She had gotten halfway out of the parking lot before she remembered that Cordite was out of chicken jerky. Marberger's was already closed for the night. She could wait until morning, or she could work up her nerve and go to the ShopStop.

Her parents had opened the place. Her dad was working the evening shift on that Friday night, like he usually did. Everything had been normal.

Until it wasn't.

Nobody knew what had really happened that night. A customer, one of the chaperones from the Homecoming Dance, had stopped in for ice and found Trey Donovan slumped over the counter, dead. PC had not stepped inside the shop since then. Her mother had sold the store to a Vietnamese couple, who'd turned out to be Hiro Tran's grandparents.

PC was sure they did a wonderful job with the store. But she got chills every time she drove past it. She decided that she'd just go to Marberger's in the morning. She was too tired and too stressed to work up the resolve to step inside the ShopStop.

When she got home, Terry was sound asleep, stretched out on the couch. Rose sat in her recliner, watching TV.

"Oh, honey. Glad you're back. Did you get your errand taken care of?"

PC hung her keys on the little hook near the door. "Sure did. And I ran into Drew. That's why I'm so late."

"Oh! That's good to hear. Honey, I hate to be a bother, but I'm out of ibuprofen. With all the goin's on this mornin', I plum forgot to ask you to get me a bottle. I've got an awful headache. Could I get you to run out and get me some?"

PC took her keys back off the hook. "Sure, Mama. Be back soon."

She grumbled to herself all the way out to the car. PC was exhausted and emotionally drained. Hope was just making her place in the family, and now every indication pointed to her being a killer. Sure, PC had theories about other people who could have done it, but the only evidence led to her niece.

The truck stop was fifteen minutes away. The ShopStop was five. Which should she choose? A fifteen-minute round trip or a forty minute one? PC wasn't sure she could stay awake another forty minutes. Her eyelids had gotten frighteningly heavy coming back from Jillibella's.

ShopStop it is then. It'll be fine. The Trans take great care of it. Dog treats and ibuprofen—I'll be in and out and back home in no time.

The ShopStop parking lot looked the same as it always had. Her hands still shook as she closed the car door. She sucked in a deep breath. Then another.

"You gonna stand in the parking lot all night?"

PC's head whipped around to see Woody was coming up on her left. She didn't see his Tahoe. Must have walked from his mother's house.

"I haven't… I haven't been here, not since…"

"I'm sorry."

PC turned to look him in the eye. He seemed sincere enough. She noticed his cheekbones were sharper and his hair was thinner. The years were creeping up on him, too, she supposed.

He walked her into the mini-mart. It was well lit, and the shelves boasted the latest and greatest snacks. Woody headed to the cooler, and PC was on the same aisle, searching through the limited selection of pet items.

The cowbell clanked as the door swung open.

Are they always this busy on a Saturday night?

"Give me all the cash! Now! Move it! If you hit that alarm, you're a dead man."

Chapter 7

PC FLUNG HERSELF to the floor. She looked up into the anti-theft mirror. A scrawny male in a ski mask pointed a sawed-off shotgun at the teenage cashier through the opening in the plexiglass that was meant for the exchange of money or credit cards.

"Open the register! Now!"

Woody, who was still in uniform, had drawn his weapon and concealed himself behind a shelf of automotive products. He was outgunned and pellets from the robber's gun would cut through the thin metal like butter. Woody's vest would protect his body, but not his head.

There was no way to tell what frame of mind the masked robber was in. Clearly, his adrenalin was up, but was he adulterated in any way? She'd seen people on PCP break a leg and keep running.

The cashier, who couldn't have been older than sixteen, was blubbering. He couldn't get the register open because he was so terrified. The gunman kept screaming at him.

PC texted Tran. "10-65 at ShopStop. Need backup"

She didn't silence the phone quickly enough. The chime of Tran's reply made the felon stop and look around.

Each footfall of his boots on the hard floor rang out like a gunshot.

He took a few steps toward Woody, swiveling his head. Listening.

PC held her breath, willing the robber to stop. *Don't look across to the mirror. Turn around.*

Over the thunder of her pounding heart, she heard a squeak of rubber on tile, then the sound of a slamming door and the clack of a deadbolt lock turning.

The cashier had used the distraction to flee to the back office and lock himself in. The felon couldn't get past the plexiglass to the register or the cashier. He roared in frustration and let what was left of the shotgun's barrel point at the floor as he pounded on the plexiglass with his free hand.

Woody stepped from behind the shelving, pistol raised. "Drop. The gun." His voice was calm, but commanding.

The robber turned toward the police chief. With his face covered, it was impossible to read his expression. Impossible to predict what he might do.

He and Woody stared at each other. Neither moved.

The man in the mask laughed. His whole body shook.

Time dilated, and PC watched in slow motion as he started to raise the gun. *Why doesn't Woody pull the trigger? He's about to die.* "Shoot! Shoot!"

The tension snapped like a rubber band and time rocketed forward. The criminal wheeled toward the sound of her voice. He stood at the head of the aisle. She and Woody were at opposite ends of the next aisle over. Behind the shelving, Woody was less than five feet away from the robber.

She grabbed a roll of duct tape and threw it at the bandit. He ducked. She pelted him with anything she could grab.

Bottles of 10-W-30.

Screwdrivers.

Battery terminals.

Rawhide dog bones.

Cans of cat food.

Her aim wasn't great, but it was close enough for him to turn away and use one arm to protect his head.

Hurry up, Tran. I'm running out of stuff.

She was down to hanging air fresheners and a pet nail clipper.

"Down on the floor! Do it!" Tran yelled as he and three other officers in tactical gear burst through the front door while another two came from the hallway to the storage area.

The robber raised his arms above his head. Woody stepped up to relieve him of the shotgun.

"I know the drill." The man in the mask laid down on his belly and put his hands behind his back. An officer cuffed him and peeled off the ski mask.

PC cringed. *Worst case of meth mouth I've ever seen.*

Tran grasped her shoulder like an eagle grabbing a salmon, and she winced. "Are you okay?"

"I'm good."

He gave her a hard pat on the back and trotted to Woody.

She stood alone while the cops talked. Tran persuaded the cashier to come out of the back office, then took a statement before sending him home for the night. PC's entire body was shaking, and she felt so brittle that if anyone spoke to her, she would shatter.

Was the ShopStop cursed, or was it her?

She had to get out of there. Couldn't stand to stay another second. She rushed outside and leaned against her car.

She'd have to give her account of the failed robbery. But not now. She couldn't get through it now. And she couldn't go home either. Rose would sense something was wrong. And how could PC tell her she'd narrowly escaped the same fate as her father?

She was a mess and didn't know what to do. PC got in her SUV and started driving, not sure where to go, other than away from the ShopStop. Justice Avenue led to Business 720. She was at the truck stop. Go in and get the ibuprofen? No. Too many people. She turned around in the parking lot of the Best Southern hotel and headed back into town, then turned down random streets.

After a while, she found herself on South Cumberland. She approached the Greek Revival style house, its bold Doric columns highlighted by the light coming from the glass panes around the double front door. The streetlight stained the sidewalk a dull orange. PC parked in front. There was a car she didn't recognize in the driveway. She got out her phone and sat there, feeling as if she were suspended in time.

Finally, she texted, "Got any ibuprofen?"

A few minutes later, the front door opened, and Drew strolled down the walkway toward her. She unlocked the door.

He opened it, and the grin fell from his face. He set the bottle of pills in the cup holder and got in the car, pulling the door closed behind him. "What's happened? You look like you've seen a ghost."

She gave a bitter laugh. "I almost *was* a ghost."

He sat quietly with her, giving her time to gather herself.

PC shook her head and kept her eyes forward. "I'm still trying to process what happened. I've finally quit shaking. Mostly."

"Okay."

PC tapped the bottle. "How did you know I was out here?"

"Doorbell camera."

PC nodded. "Figures. Mama needed ibuprofen." PC pulled air deep into her lungs. She felt like she was standing on the edge of the high diving board. "I went to the ShopStop. There was… a robbery attempt."

Drew sucked in a breath. "Oh, wow." He laid a hand on her shoulder.

She reached across her body and covered his hand with her own, then nestled her chin on her wrist. The detective would have been happy to sit for a while in the orange glow of the streetlight, basking in Drew's comforting touch, but fatigue was replacing the adrenalin in her system. She lifted her head and slid both hands into her lap. "I don't know if you're aware, but my parents opened the ShopStop. When I was a junior in high school, my dad was killed there. Robbery. Never solved."

He touched her hair. "So, your whole life has been about trying to right that one wrong? Catch the killers. Lock them up. But you're still looking for that primal offender, the one who changed your destiny."

"What are you, Zoltar, the fortune teller?"

He squeezed her shoulder. "Degree in psychology. I've made a career out of understanding people."

"Selling art or insurance?"

"Yes."

PC almost laughed. She wasn't quite there yet, but she was getting close. "Thanks." She reached over and gave Drew's hand a squeeze. "I, uh, should probably take the ibuprofen to Mama. She was feeling pretty rough, and I've been gone a long time."

He smiled, his normally white teeth a mercury-vapor-orange. "You know I l... live so close to you. You can borrow anything, any time."

"Any time you want to borrow Guinevere, you're more than welcome." PC regretted saying that as soon as it came out of her mouth. *Why had she said such a dumb thing?*

"I'll keep that in mind, next time my grass needs mowing."

PC closed her eyes and exhaled. "I'm sorry. I didn't mean to be so flippant."

Drew opened the door. "Trauma tends to short-circuit the brain." He got out of the car and stood there, looking into the SUV. "If you want to talk some more, I'll be up for a while. Omar is asleep on the couch—he wasn't going to make it up the stairs. After you drop the ibuprofen off for Rose, we could sit out on the patio and have a glass of wine or something."

"I would love to do that. But with everything that's going on with Hope... I just feel I need to be with my family. I insist on a raincheck, though."

He smiled. "Of course. I guess we'll play it by ear for darts on Wednesday?"

"Yeah. Arraignment's tomorrow morning, so we should have a better idea then. Thanks... Thanks for listening."

He smiled. "Drive safely, and I hope Rose feels better soon." Drew shut the car door and stood on the sidewalk.

PC gave him a little wave and pulled away from the curb. It only took her five minutes to get home.

Her stomach lurched when she saw Uncle Raymond's car in front of Rose's house.

Chapter 8

ROSE LOOKED UP from her recliner. "Primrose! Where have you been? We were just about to call out a searching party."

She handed her mother the pills and reached down to scoop up Cordite. He squirmed a little, then licked her ear. PC turned to the man sitting on the couch between Rose and a drowsy Terry. She heard food prep sounds coming from the kitchen. "Uncle Raymond? What's going on?"

He picked up some sheets of paper. "Got the autopsy report this evening."

PC took the proffered pages. "What am I looking for?"

"The angle of the stab wound indicates the killer was likely taller than six feet."

The detective found the entry and read it. "How tall is Hope? 5'3"? 5'4"? This is great news! Unless there was a box she was standing on, she probably didn't do it."

But I can think of one person taller than six feet who had means and opportunity.

"Yes. Not exactly exculpatory, but it certainly casts doubt. I think we have a good shot at getting her bailed out on Monday. I doubt Travis Bailey will push a homicide charge right now. Most of his evidence is circumstantial, and Hope has no motive. Plus, there were at least five other people in the museum who potentially could have done it."

PC handed the report back. "Right. And how many of them are over six feet?"

Raymond raised an index finger. "Only one: Branislav Golob."

The detective stifled a yawn. But she was well aware that she was too tired to sleep. "Yeah. I've seen that guy in action. Seems to have some anger management issues. Is that, and the stab wound analysis, enough to make him a viable suspect? Pretty circumstantial. It's even possible that another tall someone that we don't know about was in the building."

"It may be enough to cast a shadow of doubt on Hope's guilt."

Terry stretched. "If you guys are going to hold a planning session, I'm heading home. I'm beat."

Rose leaned forward and reached out. "Get some sleep, honey. We'll pick you up in the mornin'."

He squeezed her hand, then leaned over and kissed her on the head before he left. PC took his spot on the couch next to Raymond. Rocky came into the living room with a tray of sandwiches and set it down on the coffee table.

"We probably need plates, honey." Rose sat up and closed the footrest.

"Okay, Mama. I only have two hands." Rocky wore an undershirt and boxers. Uncle Raymond must have rousted him out of bed when he arrived.

PC's brother disappeared into the kitchen and returned moments later with four plates and a roll of paper towels.

The detective put a sandwich on a plate and reached over her uncle to give it to Rose, then took one for herself. "If you want to cast some doubt, I have a few other contenders, even if they aren't taller than six feet."

Raymond nodded, his mouth full of food.

"First of all, the Golob sisters didn't seem too upset about Melanie's demise. Why was that? Because they killed her? Although neither of them is over five feet tall, much less six."

Rocky wiped his mouth. "And they're both three days older than God. Melanie should have been able to fight them off."

"Watch it!" Rose raised her sandwich for a bite.

"Sorry, Mama."

PC swallowed. "Is there any relationship between Melanie and the fact that Cvetka's credit card was found in Hope's pocket?"

"No." Raymond shook his head. "Cvetka had asked Hope to go to the City Café and buy breakfast for the employees."

"Good. Hope said that the sword was in her hand and blood got on her clothes because she took the blade from Melanie, who then collapsed, and Hope tried to catch her, getting Melanie's blood on her. Cvetka gave her the card. Any explanation for the peacock brooch?"

Raymond set a bread crust on the plate. "None."

Rocky gestured with his sandwich. "I'm sure that Branislav guy did it. Who else could it have been?"

"Well," PC said. "There were at least two other people. Omar Schmidt—"

"The man who owns Dollarmore?" Rose interrupted.

"Yes, Mama. He was dating Melanie, and he thought she was cheating on him with Branislav, so he broke it off with her. She called him to patch things up, and they were supposed to have lunch. But when Omar called her because he had to reschedule, Bran answered. Omar told me he phoned Melanie at 8:30, so he had plenty of time to get to the museum."

"There you go!" Rocky slapped the table.

Raymond leaned against the back of the couch. "Interesting. What about the other one?"

"Well, this one's a little more oblique. Jill Franco catered a meeting on Thursday at the museum, and Jagoda's check bounced." PC shrugged. "What if Melanie was running interference for Jagoda and Jill got frustrated or felt threatened? Who knows? But she did go to the museum between 8:30 and 8:45 to talk to Jagoda."

Raymond absently tapped his thumb on his thigh. "You talked to both of them?"

PC nodded.

"Did either of them see anything unusual?"

"Jill said she noticed an 18-wheeler behind the building, but she claims the front door was locked. Omar said he just hung up. If he drove over to have it out with her, he didn't admit to it."

Rose leaned forward. "Omar is probably right around six foot. I remember when he first moved to town. It was kinda at the beginning of the dollar store boom. Funny man."

"I think Branislav is the most likely suspect." Raymond stood up and retrieved his phone. "I'm going to call Michael right now and tell him about Jill and Omar, then I'm heading home. Need my beauty rest for court."

PC made a strategic exit to her bedroom. She didn't want to hang around and be asked what had taken her so long to get ibuprofen. Cordite sat on the end of the bed and whined.

"I'm sorry Cordie. Wait just a little bit more until Mama and Rocky go to bed."

PC studied the photocopied pages of her father's murder book. She hadn't felt like she'd made an iota of progress the whole time she'd been in town. There had been no plexiglass protecting the cashier when her parents owned the place. The Tran family had painted bright colors on the walls and done a few updates and modernizations, but the place didn't look significantly different today than it had forty years ago.

The detective heard Rose and Rocky telling each other goodnight. She'd wait a few more minutes, giving Rocky time to go to the bathroom and brush his teeth, then she'd take the dog out for his late-night potty break.

She turned another page. There was a photo of a blurry reflection of the back of someone's head in the anti-theft mirror. Unfortunately, the head was covered with a hoodie. The fisheye distortion made it even harder to get an idea of the person's body type.

Rocky's door closed, and she took Cordite out. After they came back in, she flipped through sheet-protector-covered pages of the death investigation until her eyelids refused to stay open. She stowed the binder and turned out the lights.

Exhausted as she was, she lay in bed with her eyes closed for what felt like hours, unable to settle into sleep. Cordite snoring beside her didn't help. Finally, fatigue overcame her.

It started out the way it always did. PC was in the supermarket, doing her grocery shopping. She stood in front of a bin of fresh peaches. The lady next to her picked up some bananas, and

PC recognized her as one of her first cases. She had been a pretty blonde lady until her boyfriend strangled her.

Running away from them wouldn't help. It never did.

The man unloading avocados from a crate looked up. Part of his head was missing. She remembered him, too. Like always, panic rose in her body. Every single person in the store was a homicide case she'd worked on.

Looking down to avoid their mangled faces or bodies, she pushed her cart toward the checkout. There at the register was Trey Donovan. Blood soaked his shirt, but otherwise, he was still the handsome young father she remembered. Rocky looked just like him.

Trey was talking, but she couldn't quite understand what he was saying. It was like he was under water, trying to speak.

PC sat bolt upright in bed, gasping for breath. She felt tears on her cheeks. Cordite tried to lick her face, but she hugged him until he squirmed. Her FlitBit said it was 3:03 AM. There was no chance of more sleep tonight.

During the arraignment on Monday morning, Hope had only been charged with the theft of the brooch, which she vigorously denied. Darla paid her bail and the whole family, plus Michael Barnsdale, walked across the park to the Brisk Rib for lunch. PC struggled to stay awake, taking frequent sips of iced tea, hoping the cold liquid and micro-doses of caffeine would keep her awake just a little longer. Seven of them sat at a round table. PC was nearly opposite of Hope, who was bookended by Darla and Michael Barnsdale.

Barnsdale cut a piece of sauce-drowned brisket. "How did the brooch come to be in your pocket?"

Darla's perfectly plucked eyebrow arched. "This can't wait until after lunch?"

"I have an appointment in forty minutes."

Hope picked at her potato. "I don't know where it came from. I've never seen it before."

"I asked the Golob sisters about it. They said they would check their records to see if it was a piece owned by the museum. But I think a jury may find it difficult to believe that a valuable antique pin made of sapphires and emeralds materialized in your pocket."

Silverware clattered to Darla's plate. "Are you accusing my daughter of lying?"

"No. But you need to understand that juries tend to be skeptical of magic. Sometimes it's better to make a plea deal than risk going to court."

Hope went as pale as her potato.

"Now look here!" Rocky stood up. "Hope didn't steal nothin'!"

Barnsdale calmly sliced his food. "Bear in mind that just because they haven't charged her with murder *yet*, doesn't mean they still won't do it. I have a private investigator looking into the museum owners' and Melanie's backgrounds—to shake the bushes and see what pops out. It's my job to give Hope the best defense possible, and I will certainly do that. Are you aware that the DA is grooming himself to run for governor?" He put the bite of meat into his mouth.

"And what does that have to do with anything?" Darla snapped.

Rocky sat back down, arms crossed.

Barnsdale swallowed. "It means he wants to appear tough on crime, so he will be aiming to get a conviction, regardless of whether she's guilty."

"But that's not right!" Rose protested.

"I agree with you; nonetheless that's the situation we find ourselves in. Violent crime has been up everywhere, even in Possumwood. You may recall that the getaway driver from that spate of armed robberies is still on the loose, and I'm sure that will color Bailey's decisions." He raked some coleslaw onto his fork.

PC's head was so heavy she could barely hold it up. She propped her elbows on the table, interlaced her fingers, and rested her chin on her hands. Her eyelids felt like sandpaper. If she could just close them for a moment...

"Primrose?"

The chair shuddered beneath her. Her body tensed, then her consciousness drifted out of the black ocean of sleep.

Raymond was shaking her shoulder. "Are you okay?"

PC yawned. "I didn't sleep well last night." She looked around. Barnsdale was gone.

"Apparently not."

Rocky snickered. Darla was stroking Hope's hair. Rose was staring at the remaining half of her barbeque sandwich.

"How about I get some to-go boxes?" PC stood up and headed for the counter. Her phone vibrated in her pocket.

It was a text from Tran. "Come in. Need your statement." There were three other messages from him that she'd missed.

PC replied. "Be there in a little while"

They packed their leftovers and left the restaurant. Hope's things were still at Rose's house, so everyone drove there first. Hope and Darla decamped to Rachel's house. PC could barely function, so she took a one-hour nap before going to the police station.

When she arrived, Annie was working the front desk. "Hey, PC! Are you okay? Hiro told me what happened last night. Everyone's kinda shook."

"Good description. I'm okay. Shook, but okay."

"If you need a tea for your nerves, my dad has a huge selection of herbs and stuff."

"Thanks. I'll keep it in mind."

Annie buzzed PC through the security door. The detective found Tran in his cube. "Hey. I was getting worried when you didn't reply to my texts."

PC sat in the chair from the next cubicle over. "Sorry. I'd put my phone on silent and forgot to change it. How are your parents holding up? That must have been a terrible shock for them."

"Yeah. Nothing like this has ever happened to them the whole time they've run the store. Or me. You and the chief…"

"Are still here. Thanks for being the cavalry."

Tran's cheeks reddened. "You ready?"

He recorded her statement, then Henrietta typed it. PC read and signed it.

The detective stood up. "I'll probably come in Thursday to work on cold cases. See you later."

PC sat in her car in front of the police station. She had to figure out where the brooch came from and who really killed Melanie Novak. There was no way she would let that smarmy Travis Bailey railroad her niece. In fact, it seemed much more likely that the killer was Branislav Golob, given the stab wound angle, the fact that he'd demonstrated poor impulse control, and that he may or may not have been having an affair with Melanie.

But could she prove it?

Chapter 9

PC HAD FED the animals and was wielding the manure fork to load the wheelbarrow. She'd gotten dexterous enough with it to pick up a single stray nugget without spilling those already resting on the tines.

A diesel engine rattled, and PC raised her head. Justice Johnson was backing her truck up to the side gate to collect the manure for her mushroom farm. The detective scooped the last pile into the wheelbarrow and rolled it over to the gate. She could just pour it straight into Justice's jute bag, saving work for both of them.

Rose's wiry friend climbed out of the cab of her black truck, whistling and carrying a pile of sacks.

PC opened the gate. "You're in a good mood this morning."

"I am indeed. You remember my neighbor, Ben Masters, right?" Justice opened the tailgate.

"How could I forget him? I thought he was going to kill us."

"I told you he was just misunderstood." Justice fitted the opening of one bag around the wheelbarrow. "Well, his parents bought an organic berry farm in Oregon. He's movin' out there to run it for 'em. He's sellin' me his property, cheap."

"So, the old family farm is re-united. That is good news." PC shook the wheelbarrow handles to encourage the last of the load to slide into the sack. "What are you going to do with the place?"

Justice sealed the sack with a zip tie. "Well, Ben worked real hard to get that food forest up and runnin'. I'll keep that, for sure. Might fence off some of the pasture for the goats. I showed you my Cashmere goats, right? I bought some Angoras, too. That little cabin he built might be a good rental during the festivals."

"Sounds like you've got it all mapped out."

"Yeah. I had to get some surveyors in to make sure the plat's accurate. Don't think it's been surveyed since Granddad sold it during the Depression, and property lines may have gotten a little wiggly in all that time. Anyway, they'll be out sometime this week. I believe there's several jobs in the county they was gonna do."

"I'm excited for you. I'll tell Mama. Bet she'll want a tour."

They finished filling the bags and Justice left.

Rocky got home from work a little after 10:00 PM. He'd pulled a double shift because several people had called in sick. Cordite gleefully met him at the door and he bent to pet the dog.

When he stood up, he looked at his sister. "Mama already gone to bed?"

"Yeah. About fifteen minutes ago."

"Listen. I'm starved. I got a text from Hope on the way home, and I'm goin' to pick her up and go to the truck stop. You wanna come?"

PC nodded. "Yes. I've been wanting to talk to her."

"I thought you might. Between Darla and her lawyer, her time's been spoken for since she got out of jail. You mind drivin'? I'm whooped."

PC picked up some papers and grabbed her keys. "We can also talk about the preliminary report on the Golobs that I got from Barnsdale this afternoon."

Hope frowned at the oversized menu. "Is there anything on here that isn't deep, chicken, or pan fried?"

"Ice cream?" PC suggested. But she was having the same struggle.

"They probably have that, too. I just haven't gotten to the back page yet."

Rocky patted his folded menu on the table. "A little grease is good for you, now and again."

Hope looked up at him, then her eyes strayed toward the hostess stand. She started waving. "Darrell! Come sit with us!"

PC looked over her shoulder and recognized the truck driver from Meadowlark Moving. He sauntered over to join them. Hope got out of the booth to give him a hug, and he gave her a little peck on the top of her head and a lop-sided grin.

He doesn't seem that tall until he's standing next to Hope.

"It's good to see you, girl. Didn't know you'd been sprung. How're you holding up?" He slid into the booth next to PC.

"I'm hangin' in there. Jail wasn't as bad as it could have been. I didn't have any cellmates, so there's that. Darrell, this is my dad, Rocky Donovan, and my Aunt PC." She gestured toward the trucker. "This is Darrell Leidecker."

Rocky half-rose to shake his hand.

PC scooted a little closer to the wall. "I remember you from the museum on Saturday."

Darrell nodded. "I thought you looked familiar."

PC wasn't enthused about being blockaded in the booth, but she was interested in talking to Darrell. "You must stop at the Slovenian Museum a lot to have gotten acquainted with Hope."

"Yeah. About once a week." Darrell rested his rough hands on the table.

The server came and took their orders.

After she left, PC pressed the issue. "So, Darrell, you also probably know Branislav and Melanie pretty well, too."

He nodded and leaned back against the seat. "I had some interactions with them. Melanie is the one who packed the crates and created the manifests, so I didn't see her that much. Bran usually came out to… supervise loading the boxes on the truck." He'd clawed his fingers to make air quotes when he used the word 'supervise.'

"That must have been annoying."

"Not really. He was an okay guy. Had a hair trigger, though." Darrell unwrapped his silverware, then patted his left hip. "But I never worried. Geraldine goes everywhere with me."

Rocky stared across the table at him. "Geraldine?"

"She's a 44 Mag Desert Eagle."

PC hadn't noticed it when she'd seen him in the museum, but when she leaned towards the table, she could see a lump under his shirt at his beltline.

Hope cocked her head. "I've been thinking about getting a gun since Aunt PC nearly got killed at the ShopStop."

"Probably best to wait until that potential murder charge gets resolved." PC took a sip of water.

Rocky paled. "Your grandfather was killed in a robbery. He had a Colt Python under the counter at the store. Didn't do him no good."

PC steered the conversation back to the more recent murder. "So, Darrell. How would you describe Branislav and Melanie's relationship?"

"Tragic."

Hope piped up, "It's true. He was head over heels for her, and she didn't really like him much. She was going out with someone else."

"Really." PC nodded to encourage more revelations.

Hope glanced at Darrell before she answered. "She always avoided being alone with him if she could. I ended up helping on projects she didn't actually need help with, just in case he came in. And…" She gestured with her index finger. "Now that you mention it, they got into a big fight on Thursday."

Rocky leaned forward.

PC pursed her lips. The one time she didn't have her notebook… "What was it about?"

Hope sighed. "I don't know. It was in Slovene."

Darrell reached across the table and patted her hands. "That's bad luck."

"Did he appear threatening?" PC fiddled with her tea spoon.

Hope hugged herself. "He appeared threatening just by walking into a room."

The detective turned to her seatmate. "How about you? Ever see any interactions between them?"

"As I said, Miss Melanie didn't get involved much with the loading. I usually got the manifests from Bran. I will say the few times I saw them together, they were like oil and water. He put his hand on her shoulder once, and she slammed her heel into his instep. Never saw him do it again."

"Interesting. What kinds of things did you typically ship for the museum? A trip a week sounds like a lot."

The server delivered their food.

Darrell picked up his silverware and sized up the chicken-fried steak that spanned the entire plate. "Well, you're right about that, Miss PC. I thought the same thing. But they are in a network with some other museums around the country, and they do a lot of horse-trading. Well, artifact trading. Plus, I think they buy and sell a lot of estate sale things online, as a personal business."

PC fidgeted with her fork. "The estate items and museum items are the same general type? Wonder how they keep track."

"I deliver and pick stuff up. Not my job to question it. Anyway, it's mostly paintings and knickknacks, but sometimes there's something real interesting. Had to get an insurance form for a peacock pin, since it was made of sapphires and emeralds."

Hope stopped shaking the ketchup bottle. "The one that ended up in my pocket?"

"Don't know anything about that." Darrell shoveled in a forkful of fried meat and chewed.

So that was supposed to go into a crate that Melanie didn't pack.

If Hope's story is true, about trying to catch the curator as she fell, could Melanie have put the pin in her pocket?

If so, why? Also, why didn't Melanie pack the crates? Was she stabbed much earlier than 8:45?

Or was there another reason?

PC peeled the crust off of her blueberry pie. "How well do you know the Golob sisters, Darrell?"

"Well, Miss PC, I've been working with them since they opened the place. Delivered all the stuff for their exhibits. Even before they hired Melanie and before Bran came over. It's got to be...thirteen, fourteen years now." Darrell shoveled a massive forkful of steak and potatoes into his mouth.

"How did they get along with Melanie?"

Darrell chewed thoughtfully.

"There was some definite tension." Hope said, wagging a fry. "Melanie had a lot of ideas for the place, and they didn't want anything changed. I think they should have listened to Melanie—the place could use some freshening up."

Darrell swallowed. "I agree. Generation gap, I suppose. Jagoda and Cvetka are set in their ways. Melanie wanted to modernize." He spread his hands. "There were some disagreements." He speared some green beans, then looked up sharply. "But they would never hurt her. No, ma'am. No. I have always known them to go to the back office when they first open the museum to handle emails and whatnot. And I try to get there either before opening or after closing. In fact, I was on the phone with Jagoda that morning. I called around 8:30 to give her my ETA. It was a video call, so I saw her in her office. Cvetka was there, too. She said she was sending Hope out to get breakfast and asked me what I wanted to eat."

"Nice of them to feed you. And she didn't indicate at that time that Melanie hadn't packed the crates?"

"No, she didn't mention anything about the cargo." Darrell scooped up more meat and potatoes.

The detective made a mental note to advise Tran to check Darrell's phone records, if he hadn't already. But if his story was true, then the sisters weren't involved. It hadn't been likely, anyway, given that they were scarcely five feet tall, and the killer was apparently over six.

Six-and-a-half-foot Branislav was seen arguing with Melanie, had poor impulse control, and an unrequited love for her. He definitely had means. Probably had motive and opportunity. What she needed now was evidence. She was itching to look at the PI report from Hope's lawyer, but she wasn't about to bring it out with Darrell there.

PC figured it would have taken her several days to eat that massive chicken-fried steak on Darrell's plate, but he polished it off in record time. And both side dishes. He washed everything down with most of a carafe of coffee, then he stood up and stretched before getting some bills out of his wallet to lay on the table.

"It's been real nice meeting you." He looked from Rocky to PC. "Miss Hope, hang in there, baby. I'm sure you didn't kill Melanie. One hundred percent. You have my number. Call me if there's anything I can do to help you out."

"Thank you." She squeezed his fingers. "Wait!"

Hope scrambled out of her seat, phone in hand. She stood next to him and stretched out her arm. "Smile!"

Before he realized what was happening, she'd taken a selfie. He'd raised his hand, but not fast enough to block his face.

"Miss Hope, darlin' I wish you woulda asked me first. I know you don't mean nothing by it, but please don't put me on your socials." He gave her a hurt puppy look. "I have a cousin who is crazy as a betsy bug. When our grandparents died, she didn't get what she wanted in the will and blamed me. Always gives me a lot of grief, so I try to keep a low profile. Now, I'm sure *you* aren't her friend, but there's always a friend of a friend of a friend…"

"Oh, of course. I wasn't planning to… I just wanted a picture of my buddy. You've been nothing but nice to me this whole time."

He grinned at her, then turned with a wave and started for the door. Something black fell to the ground from his pocket.

"Darrell! You dropped something!" Hope called.

He stopped and turned around, then picked up a black driving glove from the floor. "Thank you, Miss Hope. I'd be lost without these—keep my hands from goin' numb while I'm drivin'. Y'all have a good evenin', now."

Rocky's eyes narrowed as he watched Darrell disappear into the dark. "You be careful round that boy, Hope. He seems a bit too friendly, if you know what I mean."

Hope covered her eyes with her hand for a moment. "Daaad. He's just being nice. After all that Justin put me through, I'm swearing off men. At least for now."

PC waited until she was pretty sure Darrell was out of earshot. Then she retrieved the folded papers from her bag. "I'd just printed this when you got home, Rocky."

There was one page on Jagoda, one on Cvetka, and almost two on Branislav. PC doled out the sisters' pages to Hope and Rocky, while she kept Bran's for herself.

They read in silence until PC gave hers a shake.

"Oh, wow. I can't believe this!"

Chapter 10

"WHAT IS IT? What can't you believe?" Rocky set his page on the table.

Hope moved her half-eaten order of fries out of the way and did the same.

"Looks like our boy Branislav has done some time. Terms are a little different, but it looks like assault, robbery, extortion, and last, but not least, he was arrested for a murder. The charges were dropped when the only witness fell off a balcony two days before his trial."

Rocky grinned. "How about that? Maybe they'll leave Hope alone and go after him."

PC tilted her head. "While it's true that past is prologue, just because he killed someone ten years ago doesn't automatically mean he killed Melanie on Saturday. In my opinion, though, he's a stronger suspect than Hope."

"What do you mean Hope's still a suspect?" Rocky scowled.

PC shifted in her seat. The thin padding over the hard bench did nothing to keep her tailbone from going numb. "Look, Rocky. I don't believe Hope killed anybody. The problem here is that she was found with the murder weapon in hand, standing over the body. There's got to be a lot of evidence coming from somewhere that makes someone else, like Bran, more interesting to the prosecutor. Right now, we've got bupkis."

Hope sniffled.

Rocky put his arm around her shoulders. "Don't you worry. We'll get this figgered out."

PC tapped the end of her fork on the table. "I have an idea. Surely they've cleaned up all the crime scene tape by now. I'll go to the Slovenian Museum tomorrow and look around."

"I'll go with you!" Hope sat forward.

"No. That's a bad idea. They don't know *me*. If I get the opportunity to talk to the sisters, they'll clam up tighter than Santa's waistband if you're around. If they believe that you killed Melanie, how do you think they'll react to seeing you at the museum?"

Hope crossed her arms. "Fine. But I wanted to check on the girls. Could you ask how they're doing?"

PC cocked her head. "What girls?"

"Cvetka said they were foreign exchange students from South Asia. I think two were from Bangladesh and the other one was from Sri Lanka. They helped me repair some mannequins in the attic until Jagoda found out and blew a gasket."

"Why was that?"

Hope cut her eyes to the ceiling. "She claimed they were supposed to be learning English, not doing manual labor. She herded them downstairs. That was Thursday, and she had them doing stuff in the back office on Friday."

"Did it not seem odd to you that there would be foreign exchange students in the middle of summer?" PC pushed her plate away.

"Now that you mention it, it does."

"Did you see them on Saturday?"

"No."

Rocky yawned and pushed his chicken-bone-laden plate to the center of the table.

PC wondered if he was making space to put his head down. "Alright. Let's pay up and get out of here." PC slid out of the booth and stood, wincing at the pins-and-needles sensation in her backside.

Promptly at 10:00, the Museum of Slovenian Culture opened its doors. PC noted the red late model Mercedes and the black BMW parked in the 'reserved for staff' spaces. That's a lot of luncheons. She paid the $8 for her ticket and started wandering the smaller galleries on the first floor, casually making her way to the one where Melanie was killed.

The room was painted in a trompe l'oeil style. The mural wasn't especially well done—there were a number of perspective discrepancies—but it was supposed to make visitors feel they were standing in a courtyard. The painting's formal garden on one wall wrapped into what appeared to be a grand palace on the other three.

The museum's regular flooring had been replaced with cobblestones, and a dry antique fountain, surrounded by artificial flowers, anchored the center of the room. Artifacts were integrated into the mural and displayed on the walls in a mixed-media presentation.

A rack holding three swords, with a space for a fourth, hung on a wall, as if visible through a fictitious second-story window. It was high enough that PC didn't believe Hope could reach it. But it would have been easy for Branislav.

Everything pointed to Bran. Except the cold, hard evidence. That was a problem. Given the nature of the wound and the location of the sword, it seemed very unlikely that Hope was the killer, but she was the one with the sword in her hand and the victim's blood on her clothes. If she had tried to catch Melanie as she collapsed, it would make perfect sense. That might even explain how the expensive peacock brooch came to be in Hope's pocket.

PC took some pictures.

A metallic clatter and the sound of voices reached her ears before the smell of fajitas reached her nose. She stuck her head out of the gallery to see Jill Franco and half a dozen people in white aprons waiting at the elevator with loaded food carts. There were a few exhibits the second floor, mostly paintings and a couple of statues, but it was generally utilized for events.

PC casually made her way up the stairs. She'd try to catch Jill and see what had happened. Last time the caterer was fuming because Jagoda's check bounced. The detective studied paintings and *objets d'art* while she waited for Jill to get the situation in hand. Once things were set up, PC would try to bend her ear.

Turns out she didn't have to wait. Jill came over to her. "Hey, PC. Didn't expect to see you here."

"Well, after what you told me, I wouldn't have expected to see you here, either."

Jill gave a half-chuckle. "Yeah. When I got back to the restaurant on Saturday, there was a produce truck waiting on me, and it was Monday afternoon before I got a chance to talk to Jagoda. She apologized and said there was an unexpected cash flow issue, some grant money holdup, or something. We set up a bank transfer, and she's going to EFT the funds to me from now on."

PC nodded. "Cool."

"Well, I've got to get back to setting up. The Chamber of Commerce will be here in half an hour."

"Good to see you, Jill."

PC was about to head back down the stairs when the elevator doors opened and Jagoda stepped out. The detective immediately began constructing a pretext to approach her. Since she had been banned from the case, she couldn't very well just come out and question Jagoda. And the Slovenian might be somewhat hostile, given that Rocky had attacked her brother. Surely she'd recognize PC from that cringeworthy event, if not from Saturday morning at the crime scene. It had to seem like a normal, unremarkable, eminently forgettable conversation. For Jagoda.

The older woman was tapping on her cell phone, and PC sauntered over. "Ms. Golob?"

Jagoda looked up. As soon as she recognized PC, she scowled.

"Ms. Golob, I just wanted to apologize again for my brother's actions. This whole situation has been tough on our family. I imagine you must be devastated by the loss of your curator."

"Melanie was hard worker." Jagoda nodded. "We miss her."

"Yes. The whole situation is very tragic. Especially for your brother."

"My brother? How you mean?"

PC pretended to be surprised. "Oh… I thought he and Melanie were dating."

Jagoda's eyes blazed, perhaps irked by the idea of her brother being with the hired help. "You have thought incorrectly."

The detective couldn't lose her quarry like this. "I'm sorry. I didn't mean to pry. I was just… please forgive me. It must be such a comfort to you to have him around. Especially when it feels like violent crime has taken over the town."

One eyebrow arched over Jagoda's light brown eye. "Is true. He is good brother. Good protector."

"I'm sure he is. Does he help out much with the foreign exchange students you've been hosting?"

Jagoda's eyes flashed to the staircase that led to the attic. "I know of no, how you say? Foreign exchange students. Who has told you this?"

Again, the detective feigned bewilderment. "I... hadn't realized it was a secret. I'm not sure who I heard it from. Perhaps Jill mentioned it Saturday after she spoke with you...?"

Jagoda's eyes narrowed. "No. No see Jill Saturday."

"Sorry. I must be mistaken. I have enjoyed visiting the museum. Thank you for taking a moment to speak with me." PC gave her a broad smile. It's hard for people to stay mad at a thank you and a smile. Hopefully, she'd still be willing to talk to PC the next time. If there was a next time.

The detective took the stairs down to the first floor and left. She wasn't quite sure how welcome she'd be, turning up unannounced at the Possumwood PD.

She texted Tran. "I have some intel you may not have."

It took a few minutes for him to respond. "Picnic area @ City Park. 1 hour."

PC replied. "C U then"

Tran was already sitting at a picnic table when PC rolled up. He watched as she approached. "Hey. How's it going?"

PC shrugged. "It's going."

"So, what you got for me?"

The detective sat down. "Have you found the girls?"

Tran frowned. "What girls?"

"Hope told me that on Thursday that three young, South Asian women appeared at the museum. They were helping her on a project when Jagoda whisked them away to the back office. She kept them working with her on Friday, and Hope didn't see them on Saturday. Jagoda told her they were foreign exchange students."

Tran straightened. "We do get foreign exchange students in Possumwood, you know."

"In July?"

"Or not."

PC fiddled with an oak leaf that had fallen on the table. "When I asked Jagoda about the girls, she denied that there were any. They could be keeping them in the attic." The detective shrugged. "I don't know."

"First of all, why were you talking to Jagoda?"

"I was at the museum. I bought a ticket and took a tour, just like any other private citizen."

Both of Tran's eyebrows raised. "You were snooping."

"Prove it."

He chuckled. "I'd be disappointed if you weren't. So, what are you thinking? I can't just barge in there and ask to look around for three young women who may not even exist."

PC crossed her arms on the table. "They exist. Have you read the research from Hope's attorney on the Golobs?"

Tran looked down. "Not yet."

The detective sighed. "Nothing on the sisters. Branislav, however, has a record. The murder charge didn't stick because the witness took a header off a balcony before they could testify. I'm thinking Immigration might be interested in the situation."

"You think Bran is a coyote?"

"If the shoe fits. Not sure how he'd be smuggling immigrants from South Asia, but there they are. And besides, you might have noticed that the Golobs drive very expensive cars. I suppose they could be independently wealthy and decided to open a museum on a lark, but unless that's the case, I don't see how they can keep up the museum and afford fancy cars when they rarely sell more than ten $8 tickets a week."

Tran's brow furrowed. "They do host a lot of events—their venue's very popular."

"The model base price of the red Mercedes is $75,000."

Tran bit his lip.

"Anyway, I hope you're considering Branislav in Melanie's murder. Hope isn't tall enough to reach that rack of swords on the wall." PC stood up. "Thanks for meeting me."

"Thanks for the tip."

PC set a bag of six of the Biersal's famous fresh pretzels on the table and sat down on a stool next to Drew. The other darts regulars were there: Jim and Winnie Hargraves, Bill Montoya, and Mary Anne McDonald.

Jim inhaled deeply as he took a pretzel. "I'm going to have to talk to the Zimmerman boys about selling their pretzels at the café."

Winnie elbowed him. "PC, how is Rocky doin'?"

She froze for a second. Winnie wouldn't know about the concussion. It must be the Hope situation. "He's holding up. It's tough on all of us."

"Having a killer in the family's gotta be hard." Montoya slugged some dark beer.

"My niece is not a killer," PC said, each word a crisp staccato beat.

"No offense." He hastily stuffed a pretzel into his mouth.

The detective nibbled her own pretzel. It was good to have a couple of hours off and relax with friends. Bill couldn't help being Bill. He was often a little awkward, but he wasn't a bad guy.

"What are we playin' tonight?" Mary Anne asked.

Drew unzipped his darts case. "I was thinking—"

Daisy burst through the front door of the Biersal and sprinted towards PC. Which was especially shocking, because Daisy didn't run.

"PC! You've got to come quick! Now!" She tugged at her sister's arm. Mascara was smeared down her cheek and her eyes were red and puffy.

"What's happened? Is it Mama?"

"No! Branislav Golob is dead. And Hope killed him!"

Chapter 11

SILENCE SWALLOWED THE Biersal. Every eye turned toward the dartboard area. PC blinked rapidly a few times.

"What did you say?"

Daisy got closer and spoke into PC's ear. "Branislav is dead. Hope killed him."

"That's what I thought you said." She sighed. "Alright. Let's go."

PC's brain was in overdrive, scrambling to make sense of what her sister had just told her. "Come on. Daisy, where is she?"

"At the police station."

"What about Mama? Have you told Rocky?"

"Mama was tryin' to get a hold of Mr. Barnsdale. Rocky's at school—I ain't had the heart to call him yet."

"There's not really anything he can do. I think his class is done at nine. I'll call him then. Can you stay with Mama? I'll get to the station and see what I can do."

Daisy nodded and fled out the front door.

PC patted her pockets and stopped. "I didn't drive!"

Drew took her elbow. "I did. Come on."

She and Drew hurried to the back parking lot.

When they arrived at Possumwood PD, Michael Barnsdale was just getting out of his Land Rover.

PC didn't give him the opportunity to open his mouth. "What happened?"

"No idea. Rose called and said the police had arrested Hope for shooting Branislav Golob. That's all I know."

An older male officer sat at the front desk. "Can I help you?"

"Yes. You've detained my client, Hope Gladstone. I need to speak with her."

The officer picked up the desk phone and punched a few buttons. "Hey. Gladstone case. Lawyer's here."

A few minutes of stiff silence passed before Officer Sanchez opened the door. "Hey, PC. You here to work on those cold case files?" She didn't wait for a response before she looked at the two men. "Which of you's the lawyer?"

Barnsdale stepped forward. "That would be me."

She eyed Drew. "And who are you?"

"Friend of the family."

"Sorry, you're going to have to wait out here." She motioned to PC and Barnsdale to follow her.

PC turned to her friend. "This may take a while. If you want to go home, I won't be offended."

A ghost of a smile floated over Drew's lips. "I'm not gonna leave you stranded."

Sanchez took Barnsdale in to see Hope, and PC waited in the conference room until she came back. "Hey, Sanchez. What happened?"

The officer shook her head. "Her lawyer's got his hands full with this one. Somebody called in an anonymous tip around 5:30 that they saw a woman matching her description shoot Branislav Golob, put the gun under the seat in her car, and drive away. Gorman was the one who investigated the location and found the body. Chief put out a BOLO, and they picked her up pretty quick. Anyway, Golob had been shot with a 9 millimeter, and guess what was under the driver's seat? She also had gunshot residue all over her hands."

PC struggled to find something to say. "Did the ballistics match?"

"Guess we'll find out. It's been sent to the lab. Chief drove it himself."

Of course he did.

"Registration?"

"Nope."

PC shook her head. "I'm stunned, honestly. What did Ho-the suspect say happened?"

"She denied it, of course. Don't they all? She had some cockamamie story about going out in the woods to practice shooting with some truck driver." Sanchez rolled her eyes. "You just missed him, actually. We called him to verify her story. The suspect claims she met him at 4:00, but he has a loading ticket that shows him in San Antonio at 3:30."

"A truck driver. Huh. You remember his name?"

"Not off the top of my head. But the company name is something to do with a bird."

"Could it be Meadowlark Moving?"

"That sounds about right."

Darrell Leidecker. Oh, Hope. Why did you pick someone for your story that was going to have such an easily provable alibi? I'd been so sure you hadn't killed Melanie, either, but now...?

"I guess that makes Travis Bailey's job easier."

"Well, yeah. Two dead bodies. Two murder weapons covered in her fingerprints. Didn't learn from her mistakes the first time around. Can't fix stupid, I guess."

PC bristled, so she controlled her breathing to control her emotions. "Perhaps not."

But Hope isn't stupid. Or at least PC hadn't thought so. Had Branislav threatened her, and she shot him in self-defense? If that was true, why the crazy story about going shooting in the woods with Darrell, who was clearly not there?

PC couldn't help feeling there was more to it.

"How did you get in touch with the truck driver?"

"Suspect had his cell number. We called him up. After he dropped his freight in Houston, he came in and gave a statement, since he was on his way to Waco, anyway. He said he'd be staying at the Best Southern tonight if we needed anything else from him. Anyway, I got some paperwork I need to finish up. See ya."

As soon as Sanchez's back was turned, PC texted Barnsdale. "Going to follow a lead. Want to talk later."

When PC came out, Drew sat reading a book on his cell phone. He looked up when the security door opened, and she gave him a grim smile. "Let's go."

He waited until they got in his car to ask what happened. She recounted what Sanchez had told her, then pulled out her smartphone and looked up the Best Southern. She tapped the number and waited.

"Best Southern."

"Yes. Can you ring Darrell Leidecker's room for me?"

There was a pause, then the extension started ringing. And ringing. PC was just about to hang up.

"Hello?"

"Mr. Leidecker?"

"Who's this?"

"PC Donovan. I'm Hope's aunt. We met at the Fast Fuel the other night."

He hesitated. "Yeah, I remember."

"Could we talk?"

"I… don't know if that's a good idea."

PC tapped her thumb on the dashboard. "I understand why you might be reluctant. But I really need to get some things straight in my head. It would be a huge help if you would give me a few minutes of your time."

He waited so long to reply that PC wondered if he was still there. "Okay. I'm going downstairs to the Silver Dollar. I'll be there for a while."

"Thank you, Mr. Leidecker."

PC hung up and Drew started the car.

"Where're we going?"

"Silver Dollar Saloon."

PC thought she glimpsed a look of horror pass over Drew's face, but it could just have been the lengthening shadows of the encroaching twilight.

"Am I correct in guessing that Mr. Leidecker can be found there?"

"You are."

The Best Southern Motel had lost its sparkly new shine decades ago. PC was a kid when it had been built, and they sold pool passes for $10 a month for unlimited swimming. She, Rocky, and Daisy had spent a lot of hot summer afternoons there, and she felt a twinge of sadness at how badly the place had gone to seed. They passed the cracked terra cotta stucco walls and stepped inside. To their right was the check-in desk with its greasy clerk and the shabby breakfast nook.

They turned left. Lurid blue and red neon made the dim amber light in the cavernous bar somehow even more sickly and sallow. A silent jukebox squatted in the far corner. Two men aggressively played foosball next to a vacant pool table with a rip in the felt. A small group played cards at a corner table. The few women in the place were surrounded by men, and PC could understand why Daisy would come here if she was looking for attention. Darrell Leidecker sat at the bar, three-quarters of a glass of beer next to him, scanning through screens on his phone.

As she and Drew walked through the bar, PC felt eyes on her, judging her, evaluating whether she was a good prospect for a conquest attempt. She felt dirty, as if grime from the cigarette smoke-stained walls was falling on her and seeping into her skin.

"Hey, Darrell." She gave him a half-hearted smile.

He looked up and nodded at the two of them.

PC cleared her throat. "This is my friend, Drew. Drew, Darrell."

An impish grin crept across Darrell's mouth. "Miss PC, you didn't have to bring a bodyguard. Place may be a dive, but it's not dangerous."

The detective tried to match his tone. "Well, we were already out when I got the call about Hope." She pulled out a barstool and sat down.

Drew did the same.

Leidecker picked up his glass and shook his head. "Poor Hope. She seemed like such a nice kid. Terrible shame about Bran. I don't know why she tried to involve me." He sipped his beer.

PC propped an elbow on the bar. "Well, you did say you're always armed, and she mentioned wanting to get a gun."

The trucker shrugged. "If she would have asked me, I would have given her shooting lessons. But not with Geraldine. I think a 44 Mag is too big for somebody as little as Hope—a Glock or a Beretta 9 mil is a better fit for her. Don't suppose that matters, now."

"No. Probably not. Did Hope say anything to you about Branislav? She seemed to be intimidated by him."

Leidecker shook his head. "Why do you think she talked to me about him?"

"When you left the truck stop, you told her to call you if she needed anything."

He rocked back and forth slightly. "So I did. But if she was planning to permanently solve any problems she might have been having with Bran, she didn't discuss it with me."

Drew leaned over PC. "What time did you say you picked up your load in San Antonio?"

PC elbowed him back into his place.

The driver ran his tongue over his teeth. "Well, if you must know. Picked up in San Antonio at 3:30 dropped off in Houston at 6:45. Stopped at Brandee's to grab a bite before I headed to Waco. You can ask for the security cam video." An unattractive smirk curled his mouth. "That's when Possumwood PD called me. And I gave them the receipts."

Leidecker swirled the beer around his glass. "Sure feel bad about Miss Hope. Maybe she can get some professional help for her, I don't know if you want to call them delusions or hallucinations. I really liked her."

PC made a noncommittal *mmmm*.

Someone started the jukebox, and it blared a Jimmy Buffett song. PC felt like she was wasting away in this bedraggled bar.

The bartender finally made it over to where they sat. "What'll it be?"

Drew shook his head. "I'm good."

PC gave the man a tight smile. "We were just leaving. Thanks."

He shrugged and drifted back to the other end of the bar.

"Thanks for your time." The detective slid off her stool.

Leidecker nodded and raised his beer in salute before putting it to his lips.

She and Drew headed for the exit. As soon as they got outside the motel, PC breathed deeply to chase the stale air out of her lungs.

"What do you think?" Drew asked as they walked to his car.

"He's got documentation that he wasn't in Possumwood when the murder happened. He kind of rubs me the wrong way with his faux folksiness, but being fake isn't illegal."

"Faux folksiness." Drew let the words slide over his tongue and trickle out of his mouth.

"Yeah. Miss Hope. Miss PC. He never called you Mr. Drew."

"True enough." He shrugged. "But what I was asking was what you think about Hope?"

"I want to believe her. You have no idea how much I want to believe her. But the evidence doesn't support her story. Someone else could have killed Melanie—Branislav was a top contender— but I'm struggling to rule Hope out in *his* death. It looks like a slam dunk."

He unlocked the doors with the remote. "You're right. This case seems to be wrapped up with a big bow. Not a single loose end."

PC got into the car. "Yeah. And I think that's what's been bothering me."

Chapter 12

DREW PULLED UP in Rose's driveway. "Do you want me to come in? If you need some moral support…"

"I would love for you to come in. But I expect there's going to be a lot of family drama, and possibly a late-night trip to the jail. I wouldn't subject you to that. Things could get… did I mention family drama?"

Speaking of family drama, I wonder if anyone has called Darla?

"It's okay. I don't want to be underfoot."

"No! That's not it at all. Unless additional evidence turns up pretty soon, I fully expect Michael Barnsdale to recommend a plea deal, which of course is gonna make Rocky hotter than ghost pepper jelly. Believe me when I say you don't want to see him like that. And I don't know where Darla is. Adding her to the mix might be… volatile."

"I think I've missed something. Who's Darla?"

"Hope's mother. It's complicated." PC ran a hand through her salt-and-pepper hair. "I should probably go. Thanks for chauffeuring me around."

He squeezed her shoulder. "It was my pleasure."

His hand was like an ember on her skin, thawing the cold dread that gripped her insides. She wanted to stay in the eye of the hurricane, the calm of his car in his presence. But she couldn't.

"Good night." PC stepped out of the car and headed into gale force headwinds of her family drama.

Cordite barked as she opened the screen door and walked across the porch. PC gathered herself before she turned the front doorknob.

Someone had, in fact, called Darla. PC almost hit her with the door as she stood talking on her cell, eyes lined with red and skin blotchy. The detective scooped up Cordite and tip-toed past her.

Rose sat on the couch, her head resting on Terry's shoulder while he stroked her hair and shoulder. They stared at her, open-mouthed, like hungry nestlings waiting for her to feed them a worm of good news.

Daisy strode out of the kitchen. "Well?"

"Has Barnsdale called yet?"

Her sister crossed her arms. "No."

PC glanced at her FlitBit. 9:27. "I don't suppose anyone's called Rocky."

Daisy tilted her head towards Darla.

"How much does she know?"

"Not enough." Darla's voice, husky with emotion, startled PC. Even Cordite flinched.

The detective sighed. "Well, it doesn't look good. PPD got an anonymous tip at 5:30, giving a description of Hope and the car she was driving."

"That's my rental," Darla said.

PC nodded. "They found the same type of gun that killed Branislav under the seat of her car, and she had GSR all over her hands."

Roses' eyes widened. "She had what on her hands?"

"Gunshot residue, Mama."

Rose put a hand to her mouth, and Terry squeezed her shoulders.

"To make things worse, Hope claims she was out practicing shooting with a truck driver named Darrell Leidecker. He has receipts to prove he was in San Antonio, picking up freight at the time."

"That's ridiculous!" Darla snarled. "Hope wouldn't hurt anybody."

"Then tell me who did?" PC hadn't meant to snap. She rubbed the bridge of her nose. "Look. I don't want to believe it either. Now, it hasn't been confirmed that the gun found in Hope's car is the murder weapon. I suppose it's possible she coincidentally had an unregistered gun of the same caliber as the one that killed Branislav Golob stashed under the front seat of her car."

Darla scowled. "Hope didn't own a gun. As far as I know, she's never even fired one."

"She was out shooting with somebody; she freely admits that. But I don't see how it could have been Darrell Leidecker. I've been trying to come up with scenarios… Hope was clearly intimidated by Branislav, and I'm fairly convinced that he was the one who killed Melanie. Maybe he came after Hope and she killed him in self-defense. But that doesn't explain her story about shooting with Leidecker."

Darla crossed her arms. "And why are you so sure he isn't the one lying?"

"Because he has loading tickets from San Antonio at 3:30 and Houston at 6:45. It's a three-hour drive, and he would still have to have the pedal to the metal to get to Houston and get unloaded in three hours and fifteen minutes. Also has receipt from snacks he bought at Brandee's Travel Plaza after he left Houston."

Darla scowled and gnawed the inside of her cheek.

Terry patted Rose's knee. "What if she was shooting with Branislav and accidentally shot him? Where were they? If she thought nobody would find the body, she could just pretend it never happened."

"Still doesn't explain why she dragged Leidecker into it."

"If they were friends, perhaps she thought he'd back her up, regardless."

PC shrugged. "Maybe. I feel like there's a lot of missing pieces, because the ones we have don't all fit together."

Gravel crunched in the driveway. Cordite's ears pricked up, then folded against his skull before he buried his face under PC's collar. The screen door on the front porch snapped against the frame. The glass in the front door rattled as it was thrown open.

"Let's go get Hope."

Darla's eyes narrowed. "Don't be such a drama queen, Rocky. You know we can't just bust her out of jail like some old TV western."

A glance at the clock told PC that Rocky was home almost fifteen minutes early. She was glad he'd made it home in one piece. "We're doing the best we can. Barnsdale is with her right now."

"This is gettin' ridiculous, I'll tell you what."

PC could almost see smoke coming out of her brother's ears. "Please don't do anything rash."

And then a terrible thought occurred to her. What if Hope was protecting someone, and that's why she lied about Leidecker?

"Hey, Rock? What kind of gun do you have?"

He looked at her as if she'd sprouted a second head. "What?"

"What kind of gun do you have?"

His face reddened.

Uh-oh.

"You know I don't do guns, Primrose. What are you getting at?"

Primrose. That was almost like Mama calling one of her offspring by all three names.

"Never mind, Rocky. Somebody was teaching Hope to shoot this afternoon, and I think she's trying to protect them. Just wanted to make sure it wasn't you."

He glared at PC for a long moment. "Would somebody please fill me in on what's happened? Darla didn't say much, other than Hope had been arrested again for another murder."

PC nodded and gestured to the loveseat. "You might want to sit down."

The detective had gotten to the part about talking to Darrell Leidecker at the Silver Dollar Saloon when Darla's phone rang. She got up and went into the kitchen.

PC couldn't eavesdrop and talk at the same time, so she finished giving Rocky the rundown.

When Darla returned to the living room, she looked defeated. "That was Michael Barnsdale. He thinks the safest plan is for Hope to plead to a lesser charge—he's trying to get the DA to go for manslaughter, although he thinks it will probably be second degree murder—but she steadfastly refuses. She swears up and down she's innocent. If she pleads not guilty and it goes to trial... he's going to have a hard time refuting the evidence against her."

"You're her mother! Why don't you believe her?" Rocky snarled.

"It. Doesn't. Matter. Whether or not I believe her. The jury is going to hear that she had the murder weapon, covered in her prints, and she had fired a gun. Do you think they'll give her life in prison, or put her on death row?"

"She didn't kill anybody!" There was less vehemence in Rocky's voice this time.

PC gave an exasperated sigh. "But we can't prove that. Without something else, Travis Bailey has an open and shut case in Branislav's death, and since he's going there, he'll probably pin Melanie's murder on her, too."

Even though she'd gone to bed at 3:00 AM, sleep had been elusive. It felt like PC had just dozed off when her phone started blaring from the nightstand. She fumbled to hit the snooze button. But it wasn't the alarm. It was a call.

"Tran? What time is it?"

"Quarter of seven. I need you to come with me. Pick you up in fifteen."

He hung up before she could protest. The detective threw on some clothes, brushed her teeth, and hurried out to serve breakfast to the critters. Cordite came with her to supervise. Tran pulled up in the driveway before she was finished putting out the hay. He could wait a minute.

Cordite barked.

"You almost done?"

Tran hadn't waited. He'd come around the house and stood at the fence. At least he hadn't knocked on the door and woken Mama up. Just activated the dog.

"Yeah. Just about. Meet me around front."

PC scooped up the agitated canine, whose pride seemed impinged upon by such an insensitive gesture, and carried him into the house. She gave him a slice of chicken jerky and washed her hands. "You look out for Mama, okay?"

The detective grabbed her bag and keys and slipped out the front.

Tran started the cruiser.

PC got in. "What's going on?" she asked as she buckled up.

"There's been a report of some prowlers at *Happily Ever Afters*."

The detective slumped against the back of the seat. "And you need me for that? I'm kinda dealing with some stuff right now." She would have gotten out of the car if he wasn't already halfway out of the driveway.

"That's why I asked you to come."

"For what? Some kind of group therapy?"

"No." Tran turned onto Travis Street. "This directly relates to Melanie's murder. At least, I think it does."

"I'm listening."

"The first thing is that when we interviewed Omar Schmidt, he told us there were some females talking intermittently in the background when Melanie had called him on Friday about meeting up. He didn't understand what they were saying, but he was really only paying attention to Melanie. He assumed she was at a restaurant or store, but then she said she was driving."

"You know he had time to get to the Slovenian Museum and kill her, right?"

"No, he didn't. He let the Dollarmore employees in at 8:45."

PC bit her lip. "What's the second thing?"

Tran waited for two cars to pass before making a left onto Second Street. "Well, you know how Ms. Gladstone insisted that there were three South Asian girls in the museum, but Jagoda denied it?"

"I remember that."

"Simone Reynolds called to report three homeless kids pilfering from the vegetable gardens at the Afters, just before dawn. She tried to talk to them, but they ran toward the pond area. And she knows that, because they disturbed the peacocks roosting in the trees as they ran under them."

I'd forgotten they had peacocks at the Afters.

PC tapped her leg. "And if it turns out that they are the girls that Hope saw, maybe they can tell us who killed Melanie."

Chapter 13

TRAN PULLED INTO the parking lot of *Happily Ever Afters*. "If they know who killed Melanie, that would be beyond helpful."

Did he doubt it was Hope? Interesting.

They got out of the squad as the infant sunrise painted the pink walls of the Victorian in an even more vibrant shade. The muggy air was heavy with the scent of old-fashioned roses. A rooster crowed in the distance. PC wondered if it was Pavarotti. She'd gotten so used to him at her mother's house that she automatically tuned him out.

Aye-yah! Yah! Yah!

PC and Tran took off running to the sound of the cries.

Was that one of the girls?

Had someone attacked the owners of the Afters?

Someone was in trouble, and PC hoped they got there in time to help.

Tran rounded the corner of the house two strides before PC, and she almost slammed into him as she turned. He stood still as an ice sculpture. In front of him, a peacock fanned his tail feathers, then shook them while he stamped his feet before a half-dozen disinterested peahens. The display ended as he curled the massive fan forward like a gothic arch. He bobbed his head.

Aye-yah! Yah! Yah!

A young woman with shoulder-length blonde hair chuckled, disturbing a white cord that ran from her ear to her pocket. "Oh, Ambrose. Give it up already. I think you have enough girlfriends." She tossed a handful of feed, and the peahens ran to her and began pecking at the ground.

Ambrose called again, but they ignored him. He seemed to sigh, then collapsed his impressive tail before joining them for breakfast. The woman threw out more food.

"Simone?" Tran unfroze and started toward her.

She glanced at her watch and raised an eyebrow before pulling the earbuds out of her ears. Then she seemed to recognize the people in her yard. "Detective Donovan. Officer Tran. I was starting to get annoyed at how long it was taking for the PPD to get here, but now I feel a lot better. We can't thank you enough for clearing our names when everybody was sure we'd tried to poison them with bad oysters. Speaking of food, did Caitlyn get that catering menu to you?"

He grinned. "Actually, Annie is handling everything for the wedding. All I have to do is show up."

"You'd better! Let me show you where I saw the kids." Simone bent to retrieve a fallen peacock tail feather and handed it to PC. "For luck."

They followed her to a series of raised beds overflowing with vegetables. Eggplants hung like obsidian pendants on sturdy stems. Cucumbers peeked at them as the breeze stirred the leaves on the trellis. Orange and red bell peppers could have been lanterns lighting the vegetable rows.

"I was getting ready to grab some peppers for the omelet bar when I looked out the window and saw figures in the garden. I came out to talk to them. Maybe they were just hungry. But they ran over to the pond. I didn't chase them—I was afraid someone might fall in and drown. I haven't seen anyone leave, and I've been keeping an eye on the front gate camera."

Tran glanced at the pond. "Could you describe them, ma'am?"

"Don't call me ma'am. Makes me feel old. I prefer Simone, but I'll take Mrs. Reynolds, if you must." She waited for Tran to nod before continuing. "There were three of them. At first I thought they were wearing hoodies, but they all three had long, dark hair. I'm guessing they were each around five feet tall, because they were standing next to the trellised passion flowers. The flowers on the ones that haven't been eaten by the gulf fritillaries are about six feet high."

"And what were they wearing?"

"I'm not a hundred percent sure. It was just getting light. But I think it was tee-shirts and jeans."

While Tran and Simone talked, PC studied the pond. Cattails grew on one side, and horsetail on another. Waterlily pads covered much of the surface, but white, purple, and hot pink flowers formed neon constellations among them. Dragonflies skimmed the water and performed acrobatic stunts high in the air.

A crushed granite path encircled the pond and led to a copse of fruit trees. Before the little grove, an ancient live oak rested its heaviest limbs on the ground. An open, faux Victorian treehouse perched on a large deck surrounded by a wrought-iron railing. The architecture was built around the massive bore of the tree, weaving over and under its ponderous limbs. PC couldn't see the ladder—must be on the other side.

The detective hadn't realized she'd started drifting toward the pond until Tran called her name.

"I'm just going to have a look around the treehouse," she called over her shoulder.

The sound of gravel shifting under her feet was oddly satisfying. A leopard frog squeaked as it leaped from the bank and splashed into the water, vanishing under the lilies. As she got closer to the big tree, she saw resurrection fern covered the tops of the horizontal branches of the oak like thick green fur. A live oak this size had to be hundreds of years old—it must have some stories to tell.

The detective walked around the massive burled trunk. The treehouse was actually supported by a wooden structure, not nailed to the tree. The bottom of the decking was probably eight to ten feet off the ground. PC climbed the wooden stairs that zig-zagged their way up to the platform. A central table with seating for eight was decorated with a mossy centerpiece that featured live orchids. In the corner opposite PC, an outdoor carpet was surrounded by a chaise lounge and oversized deck chairs, and a hammock stretched in a blue frame lay closer to the whimsical Victorian structure.

The detective stood still and listened. Nothing definitive. She admired the purple orchids as she passed and then stood at the entry to the treehouse. PC held her breath and listened again. Was it a whisper? A breath? Her imagination?

She walked into the house and turned to the left, holding the peacock feather in front of her as if it were a weapon.

The sound came again. She followed it to a built-in bench, which was basically a box that ran along one wall. Tables to set drinks on butted each end, and a third one divided the long bench exactly at the middle. The bottom of a pink tennis shoe stuck out from the box closest to PC.

"Hello?" the detective really, really didn't want to touch that shoe and find a third murder victim.

Relief flooded her as the owner of the pink tennie tried to pull it further into the hidey hole. "I see you. You can come out. I won't hurt you, I promise."

Still no reply.

PC approached the bench and tapped the shoe with her foot. "I know you're in there. Come on out."

Slowly, the other pink shoe appeared, then jeans, then a black tee-shirt. A terrified young woman with glossy black, waist-length hair cowered against the wall. When her eyes fell on the peacock feather, the tension drained from her face.

"My oh." She reached into the box, presumably to get someone's attention.

Two more females crawled out of their hiding place.

"Hello. Are you all right?" PC looked each one in the eye.

They shook their heads and whispered together.

The girl in the pink shoes spoke to PC, pronouncing her words carefully. "America is beautiful."

She has no idea what I'm saying.

The detective held her left hand palm up, as if it were a plate, and mimicked shoveling food inter her mouth. "Hungry?" Then she rubbed her belly.

All three nodded.

"Come with me." PC gestured for them to follow. They did, but hung back, giving themselves space to bolt if needed.

The light was better outside as the detective watched them climb down the stairs, and she decided that they were probably teens rather than adults. Which might seem reasonable for foreign exchange students, except for the part about them being here in the middle of summer. The closest college was about an hour from Possumwood, and the high school had no summer sessions. She'd checked.

Tran and Simone stared open-mouthed as she led her not-so-merry band of waifs down the path toward them.

PC halted. "I don't think they speak much English, but they are hungry."

"Caitlyn's cooking breakfast." She mimed eating to the girls. "Come on, let's get you some food."

They followed her around the corner, and a door creaked open, then clicked shut moments later. PC half-wished she could join them.

Tran tilted his head. "You said they didn't speak much English?"

"Or any. Makes it hard to interview them." PC looked at the garden until an idea popped into her head. "What about Dr. Chowdry? Do you think she might speak Hindi? Could also be Bengali or Sinhalese."

Or a dozen other languages from that part of the world. But those were the most common.

"I can ask her." He got out his phone and looked up her number.

PC idly twirled the peacock feather Simone had given her. Tran's back was to her as he spoke on the phone, but he turned in her direction as he hung up.

He shook his head. "She says she was born in Sugar Land. Only speaks English and Spanish fluently."

Tran looked at the grass. "Guess we should call Immigration."

"I think we should err on the side of caution. They may be garden-variety illegal immigrants, but given their age… it could be something a lot more sinister. I would call the Human Trafficking Task Force. They'll be able to get translators and we can find out what the girls know."

"That's a good idea. I'll get on it."

Once the girls had finished their breakfasts, Tran drove them to the station.

PC frowned as Tran opened the security door. "Do you really have to lock them up?"

"I can't just let them roam around the building."

"They can sit in the conference room with me while I work on cold cases."

"No. I agree—it doesn't seem fair. But there are protocols for a reason."

PC sighed. *I know.*

While Tran got them booked into a holding cell, PC strolled to the break room for coffee. As she passed by Tran's cube, she noticed a three-ring binder labeled 'Melanie Novak' and some photos lying on the desk. She checked to make sure the hallway was clear before she ducked into his office. The stack of crime scene photos didn't seem interesting, although she paused to take pictures of Darrell Leidecker's loading tickets and his Brandee's receipt. She kept thumbing through, finding nothing of note.

Until she got to the end.

The last picture was of Hope, covered in blood. PC's eyes flicked toward the hallway every few seconds as she studied the picture. The blood was smeared on Hope's clothing. There were no droplets that indicated spatter or cast-off. It looked for all the world like a contact transfer, just like Hope said. Would an expert witness be enough to cast a reasonable doubt on her guilt?

She set the photos down and checked the hallway again before she rifled through the binder. There was a particular witness statement she wanted to read.

What did you claim you were doing at the time of the murder, Branislav?

PC scanned the document. There it was: Bran was taking the trash to the dumpster just before Cvetka and Jagoda found Hope standing over Melanie's body. Karina confirmed this.

How can that *be?*

She closed the binder and continued toward her java infusion.

I'm not convinced Bran didn't kill Melanie.

She was supposed to have been there early to pack the crates, and Branislav answered her phone when Omar called at 8:30. It wasn't impossible.

One thing was for sure. She had to talk to Hope.

Chapter 14

PC's PHONE BUZZED. It was a text from Rocky. "Where are you?"

What? She looked at her FlitBit. *Oh! Hope's arraignment.*

The detective texted Tran to tell him she was leaving before she jogged across the park that separated the municipal buildings from the county courthouse. PC slipped into a seat next to Rocky seconds before court was called to order.

The judge did not grant Hope bail this time. She'd already been transferred to the county jail, but she was allowed time to consult her attorney before going back to lockup. PC wormed her way into the meeting, leaving a frustrated Rocky in the lobby. Terry took Rose home.

"Oh, Aunt PC. I'm so scared. I pled not guilty, but Mr. Barnsdale says if he can't find any new evidence before the preliminary hearing, he wants to cut a plea deal."

The attorney frowned. "Given the current evidence, I don't believe a trial will go in our favor. We still have some time to turn something up, but…"

"I didn't kill anybody, I swear. Why is this happening to me?"

PC patted her niece's shoulder. "I don't know, Hope. Sometimes things just happen. But we have a limited amount of time, and I'd really like to ask you some questions."

Barnsdale looked at his watch.

PC got out her notebook. "Ok. So, think back to Saturday. What time did you get to the museum?"

"Eight-thirty."

"Who was there?"

Hope closed her eyes. "Of course, Cvetka and Jagoda. Lance, the cashier. Karina, who does all the maintenance and so forth."

"What about Branislav?"

"He was late. I think he got there five or ten minutes after everybody else."

PC chewed the inside of her cheek. *Then how did he answer Melanie's phone at 8:30?* "What about Melanie?"

"She was already there, made a pot of coffee and everything."

"Did you actually see her?"

"Yes. She poked her head out of the gallery when we all came in. The one where she…"

"Could you tell if she was alone? Did you see or hear anyone else?"

A tear welled up in Hope's eye. "No."

A jailer came to the door. "Five minutes."

PC glanced at Barnesdale. "We're almost out of time. Tell me about yesterday."

"There isn't much to tell. Darrell Leidecker called me around ten in the morning and asked if I wanted to learn to shoot. I said 'sure,' and he told me to meet him at Fast Fuel at 4:00. I picked him up, and he navigated us out to some place in the sticks. Then we went into the woods and he gave me a lesson on how to load the gun and shoot it. He was so nice. He even gave me the gun afterward."

The detective cocked her head. "He gave you the gun?"

"Yeah. He said he'd bought it before he got Geraldine and he never used it anymore. I wasn't sure what to do with it, so I put it under the seat in my car when we left. I dropped him back at the truck stop afterwards. Mom and I were having an early dinner at *Truffles!* when the police came and arrested me. I didn't kill Branislav. I never even saw him yesterday."

Barnsdale scowled. "Hope, I can't help you unless you tell me the truth. Darrell Leidecker was picking up a load in San Antonio at 3:30, and he has proof. Sticking to this fantasy that you've concocted is only making it harder on you."

Hope started to cry.

PC rubbed her niece's arm. "Is there anyone who might have seen you with Leidecker? A cashier or someone from the mechanic shop, maybe?"

Hope shook her head. "No. I never went inside."

PC handed her a tissue. Hope dabbed at her eyes before blotting her nose. "Wait! The deer hunters! I'm pretty sure they saw us when we were shooting."

"Deer hunters?" PC picked up the damp tissue by one corner and tossed it in the trash.

"Yes. There were three of them wearing orange vests. They weren't that close to us, but I think one waved at me. He had his arm in the air."

Barnsdale sighed. "It's not deer season. I don't think it's any kind of hunting season, except for things that go year round, like rabbits."

"I saw them!" Hope's voice broke.

The jailer returned. "Time's up."

PC squeezed her niece's hand. "Hope, I know things look bad right now. But I believe you. I'll do everything I can to cut through this gordian knot. Hang in there."

Barnsdale stood in front of her and asked quietly, "Are they giving you your medication?"

She nodded.

"And you're eating?"

She shrugged.

"You have to eat."

The jailer led Hope away.

Barnsdale shook his head. "I wish you wouldn't encourage her. It's not possible that things could have happened the way she said. And now she's manufactured three deer hunters out of whole cloth." He raised his hands in a gesture of futility. "But then again, perhaps I can prove insanity."

"Mr. Barnsdale, with all due respect, I've been a homicide detective for twenty-five years. I have talked to more liars than I can count. Hope isn't lying."

"You may be right. But that means she's either hallucinating or innocent, and you have zero evidence that she's innocent."

Does being on a prescription that treats schizophrenia, bipolar disorder, and depression help Hope, or make it worse?

PC sat at the conference table at the Possumwood Police Department, and she was desperate to distract herself from the downward trajectory of her niece's situation. She pulled down a binder from the shelf.

The cold case files were colder than ever. PC stared at crime scene photos, then couldn't remember what she'd seen by the time she turned to the next one. She was fresh out of ideas on Hope's case. Actually, cases. When the translators finally arrived, maybe the girls she and Tran had found this morning would give her something to go on.

It was creeping up on lunch time when the group from the Human Trafficking Task Force members finally arrived. Tran led them into the conference room, and PC hastily shoved files back into their boxes. They spent a few minutes clarifying some questions for the team before they spoke with the girls. One translator, Swetha, spoke Sinhalese and Tamil. The other, Priya, spoke Hindi, Bengali, and Telugu. Hopefully, that would be enough.

Tran escorted PC and the task force members to the holding cell. Woody joined them there. She hadn't seen him since the attempted robbery at the ShopStop. His shirt hung off his shoulders like a droopy sail and his pants sagged, even with his belt buckled in the last hole.

Wonder what kind of diet he's on?

His eyes met hers for an uncomfortably long moment, but he didn't speak to her.

The girls appeared nervous at first, as if unsure if they could trust this new group of people.

Priya and Swetha sat on the floor of the holding cell with the girls. Swetha opened a paper shopping bag and handed an unopened package of paper plates to Priya. While she was opening the plastic, Swetha pulled out another paper sack. Once Priya handed her a plate, she retrieved a foil-wrapped package from the second bag, placed it on the plate, and passed it to the first girl, telling her to pass it along.

PC's stomach growled. Despite the foil wrap, the buttery smell of fresh paratha bread filled the room. Once everyone was served, the teens dug in with gusto. The translators ate with them and talked for some time.

Eventually, Priya stood up and approached PC and the others. "The two from Bangladesh are called Devyani and Kalindi. The Sri Lankan is Anu. They said some men came to their villages, looking for young women. They were promised jobs at a manufacturing plant." She shook her head. "I don't think that's where they were going to end up."

PC looked over at the girls. They were smiling and laughing now. *Did they realize how much danger they had been in?*

"They were smuggled in a specially designed shipping container, which was apparently picked up by a truck. Probably at the Port of Houston, but it could have been New Orleans. They aren't sure how long they were in the container before a very tall, hairy man picked them up in a parking lot in the dark."

Tall, hairy man. Branislav?

Woody leaned against the bars. "Where did he take them from there?"

"A large building. They had to walk up three flights of stairs. But it was dark, only dim lights at ankle level on the risers."

PC looked at Tran. "The Slovenian Museum?"

"Could be."

Priya continued. "There was a nice lady who took care of them. She got into an argument with the hairy man the day after they arrived at the museum. The next day, she came at night and took the girls to her house. She left for work the next morning and they didn't see her again after that."

Poor things. They must have eaten everything at Melanie's and gone foraging for food, and that's how they ended up at the Afters.

"What's going to happen to them now?" Tran asked.

"Fortunately for them, they haven't been involved in any criminal activity, so we're going to get them to their respective consulates and let them sort out the paperwork. These girls don't have any documents. Smugglers might have confiscated them, but these are very poor girls from very rural areas. They might not have had any to begin with."

"I have a question." PC shifted her weight. "When I found the girls, they were hiding in the treehouse at the Afters. The girl in the pink tennies—"

"Devyani."

"Devyani seemed afraid of me until she saw the peacock feather in my hand. Could that be some kind of code? Did the smugglers train them to follow anyone who approached them with a peacock feather? I mean, they don't speak English, so how would they know who to go with?"

Did this explain the peacock pin?

Priya laughed. "That's an interesting take, but no. They consider peacocks to be a good omen. The girls followed the sound of the peacock to the garden, where they found food, so they believed he was looking out for them. When you turned up with the feather, Devyani was certain you were there to help them."

"We found a fancy peacock brooch. Perhaps if a feather wasn't a signal, maybe the pin was."

"I can ask them if they've seen one."

"If they did, please get a description."

"Of course." Priya glanced at the girls and nodded.

PC watched the teens and translators for a few minutes longer, glad the girls were safe, before she returned to her conference table desk and sat down. She needed to think. Was there anything useful in the information the girls provided?

The detective tapped her notebook with a pen. Best get things down on paper before they leaked out of her head.

Both Hope and the teens reported a big argument between Branislav and Melanie on Thursday, but neither knew what it was about.

Branislav picked them up from the smuggler.

Melanie moved them out of the Museum on Friday.

Someone killed her on Saturday.

PC tried to integrate this information with what she already knew, and she idly twirled the peacock feather from this morning. It felt like an all-seeing eye, watching her, observing everything. What secrets could it tell her? The blue 'iris' sparkled against the dull olive circle, which was bordered in iridescent green. Round and round. She stared at the gleaming blue, almost hypnotizing herself. Then she stopped.

Of course. I know who killed Melanie and Branislav. I just have to prove it. And I think I know how.

Chapter 15

PC AND ROCKY sat at the counter at the City Café. Her half-cup of coffee had gone cold, and his cheese Danish was mostly untouched.

Rocky traced condensation on his water glass with his index finger. "What are we going to do?"

"You have the whole day off?"

"Yeah. It's Thursday. Don't have school, neither."

"Excellent. You're dressed perfectly to apply for a job at Meadowlark Moving."

"I already have a job."

"I know that, Rock. But I need some information I can only get straight from the horse's mouth, and that's the best way to get it. You don't have to accept it, if they offer. This is for Hope."

"Well, let's go, then."

"Are you sure you put the address in right?" PC frowned at the decaying house slouching on the overgrown lot bordering an industrial part of Houston.

"12039 Briar Island Drive. That's what you gave me. That's what I put in your phone."

The detective picked up her device and found a photo of Darrell's freight ticket. This was the address printed at the top of the page. Then she looked at the mailbox. The 0 and the 3 had peeled off but left ghosts of their presence behind. 12039.

Rocky folded his hands in his lap. "You s'pose there's an east and a west 12039? Maybe we're at the wrong one."

PC used her navigation app and searched for directional variants for Briar Island Drive, but came up empty. She shook her head. "Well, this is the address for Meadowlark Moving."

"Looks like they moved a long time ago."

The detective wasn't hopeful. "Could be an old address."

From the state of the house, it didn't appear to have been occupied at any time during the last twenty years. She opened a browser on her smartphone and searched for the address. "Surprise, surprise. It's a foreclosure. Bank owns it." She thought for a moment. "Rocky, get out and see if there's anything in the mailbox."

"What?"

"Check the mail."

The shake of his head said he thought she'd lost her mind. "If you say so. Hope I don't get bit by a black widow." He opened the door.

While he was gone, PC searched for 'Meadowlark Moving.'

Results returned included Meadowlark Bird, Meadowlark Lemon, and Local Movers. But no Meadowlark Moving.

The car door opened. "How did you know?" Rocky held up a package.

"Get in. We should leave."

"You want me to steal somebody's mail? It's not even addressed to Darrell Leidecker or Meadowlark Moving." He raised the package. "This here's addressed to Bo Darville."

"I'm one hundred percent sure he won't file a police report."

Rocky tossed the box onto the floor and sat down. PC pulled away from the curb before he buckled his seat belt.

"What's the rush?"

"Best not to be here when someone comes to pick up their mail."

"You said it wasn't a problem."

"I said they wouldn't report it to the authorities. It's really common for someone ordering contraband from the dark web to have it delivered to a fake name at an abandoned house. You might be surprised at how many kilos of drugs are delivered by the US postal service."

"Huh." Rocky shifted in his seat. "Now what?"

PC rolled to a stop at a light. *That's a great question, Rocky. Now what?*

"Well, the plan was to learn more about Meadowlark Moving, and we certainly did that. But now..."

I'd really like to talk to the guy in San Antonio, but there's no way to get there in time tonight. Maybe try to find the place in Houston where he offloaded?

They passed a billboard for cheap mobile phones. Beautiful, grinning couples took selfies on their affordable phones. *How many selfies have I seen Hope take?*

"Hey, Rock? Do you have Hope's phone?"

"Darla has it."

"I have an idea. Call her up and tell her we're coming."

PC, Rocky, and Tran sat at a picnic table in the city park under the shade of a bulky live oak. Even so, it was still hotter than Jillibella's 5-Alarm Chili. Birds chattered in the trees, and a group of kids kicked a soccer ball around at the opposite end of the park. When the breeze stirred, it brought a whiff of roses from the Afters across the street. The package that Rocky had taken from the mailbox earlier sat in the middle of the table.

The detective wiped sweat off her cheek before she put the phone to her ear and listened to it ring.

"Fansol Services."

"Yes ma'am. My name is Detective Sergeant Donovan. I need to speak with someone about a loading ticket for Meadowlark Moving on Wednesday afternoon."

"Hold on."

PC waited.

"This is Jerry."

"Hi, Jerry. This is Detective Donovan. Are you the one who signed the loading ticket for Meadowlark on Wednesday for three large cabinets?"

"That's me."

"Did Meadowlark pick up from you often?"

"Once or twice a month."

"If I sent you a picture of the driver that made the pickup on Wednesday, could you identify him?"

"Sure. I've been dealin' with Darrell a long time."

"Can you give me your cell number so I can text it to you?"

He gave it, and she sent the picture Hope had taken with Darrell at the truck stop. PC gave him a couple of minutes before calling back.

"This is Jerry."

"Detective Donovan again. Did you get the photo?"

"I did. But I don't know who that guy is."

That's what I thought. "Would you mind describing Darrell?"

"Sure. He's not a big guy, little less than six foot. Got a long shaggy grey beard, bald on top."

"Thanks, Jerry. I appreciate your time."

PC hung up.

"Well?" Rocky gestured erratically.

"The Darrell Leidecker who picked up the load in San Antonio is not the Darrell Leidecker who came to pick up crates from the Slovenian museum."

Rocky pulled out his phone.

"What are you doing?" PC put her hand over his.

"Callin' Hope's lawyer to get her sprung. What do you think?"

PC and Tran shared a glance, and the detective looked at the table before speaking. "Rocky, I want Hope out as much as you do. But it isn't that easy. We might have enough evidence to create a shadow of doubt for the jury, but not enough to exonerate her. At this point, we're going to need a confession from the killer."

Rocky scowled. "And how do you think you're gonna manage that?"

Tran tapped the table. "She's going to wear a wire."

"And what if he figgers it out?"

PC gave her brother a grim smile. "I'll have backup." She took a photo of the package and sent a text. "Meet me at the truck stop in 30 min."

Darrell Leidecker swaggered into the dining area of Fast Fuel. When his eyes locked on hers, his feral grin set PC on edge. But she smiled at him, anyway.

He slid into the booth and waited for her to speak.

"Afternoon, Darrell." She tapped the package on the table. "Or is it Bo Darville today?"

One corner of his mouth twitched. "You havin' a nice day, Miss PC?"

"Nice…what a word. You've pretended to be nice to Hope, then you framed her for Branislav's murder."

"That's an interesting idea. That you can't prove."

"I know you killed Melanie, too."

Darrell chuckled. "Why do you think that?"

"I'm not sure what kind of operation you and the Golobs were running. Stolen artifacts? Forged art? Doesn't matter that much. I suppose Melanie got her cut, so she went along. But when the program expanded from trafficking contraband to trafficking people, especially children, she wanted no part of it."

Darrell laughed again and flagged down a server. "Pot of coffee, Alice. And is there any cherry pie?"

Alice nodded and scurried off to the kitchen.

"And what makes you think I was in any way involved? I just picked up freight and delivered it. I'm not responsible for their criminal activities." He gave her a self-satisfied smirk.

"The peacock told me."

Darrell snorted. "You might need your medication checked."

Alice brought the coffee and pie, then topped off PC's tea before hurrying to the next table.

"You killed Melanie. The police found an expensive peacock brooch in Hope's pocket after she tried to catch the curator when she collapsed from blood loss. You said you had to get an insurance form for it, and you didn't talk about the contents of the crates when you spoke with Jagoda. She wasn't aware then that Melanie hadn't packed them. The only way you could have known about the peacock brooch was if you had seen Melanie with it."

"You're grasping at straws." He took a big bite of pie.

"No. I'm not. Melanie still arrived early at the museum. I don't know whether she was planning to confront you, or just pack the usual objects. I also don't know where she got the pin—maybe the original traffickers gave it to her so the girls would trust her, or perhaps it was serendipity. Regardless, when you found out the girls weren't there, you argued. When the door opened and the employees started coming in for the day, Melanie stuck her head out the door to wave at them. What motivated you to kill her? Anger? Trying to make an example of her?"

"That's a pretty good story you got goin' so far, Miss PC. I want to hear the rest of it." He picked up his coffee mug.

"After you grabbed the sword and stabbed her, you crept through the smaller galleries, and when everyone was distracted by finding Hope standing over Melanie, you slipped out the door and sat in your truck, pretending to be doing paperwork until you came into the museum and spoke with the police. That gave you ample time to change clothes in the sleeper part of your truck. I'm guessing you were wearing driving gloves and didn't worry about fingerprints."

"Driving gloves. Now why didn't I think of that?"

"You did. You dropped one here the other night, remember?"

His eyes narrowed for a moment. He remembered. PC could see it. Now she just needed to apply a wedge to that crack in his confidence.

"The Golobs were angry with Melanie for hiding the girls. But Branislav was in love with her. He had to have been in the small gallery with you and Melanie at 8:30, because he answered her phone to make sure she didn't tell anybody about the girls. Then he slipped out the front before Cvetka and Jagoda came in the back. He took out the trash, so maybe there was something he needed to dispose of. While he was out, you took the sword off the display and stabbed her. Branislav must have figured out that you killed her. I'm not sure how you lured him out to the woods, but you shot him with the 9 mil that you then used to give Hope shooting lessons. Pretty clever on your part, I will admit. Get her fingerprints on the murder weapon and GSR on her hands."

"If only I wasn't in San Antonio at the time." He topped off his coffee cup.

"You weren't. There was someone claiming to be Darrell Leidecker in San Antonio picking up a load, but it wasn't you. You didn't realize there was a witness when you were out giving shooting lessons."

Darrell's Adam's apple bobbed.

PC smiled to herself. *Gotcha.* "Yeah. Hope said she saw deer hunters in orange vests, but I realized they were the surveyors that were working for the county. There's a telescope built into the transit level, and the surveyor clearly saw you—could probably count the fillings in your teeth. He's said he didn't think much of it at the time, but after he heard about Branislav's murder, he came into the Mirabella County Sheriff's office and made a statement. The man he described fits you to a T."

She smiled, hoping he wouldn't call her bluff. She hadn't even remembered about the surveyors until after she'd set up the meeting with Leidecker.

He sucked his teeth, calculating. "Branislav was a hothead. Always had to clean up after him. But now it's my turn to ask questions. How did you come by this package?"

"You got sloppy and used the same address for your fake trucking company as you did for your dark web deliveries."

Darrell's hands disappeared under the table. "You know I'm armed, and if you believe I killed Melanie and Branislav, why do you think I won't kill you, too?"

"Here in a truck stop full of witnesses?"

"How much?"

"Excuse me?" PC almost knocked over her tea.

Darrell's eyes flicked at the package on the table. "You didn't hand over my goods to the cops, so you must want a cut. How much?"

"How much would you have gotten for the girls?"

"That transaction was canceled. I'm not bringing you into my organization. This is a onetime only payment. How much for you to go away?"

Stop dancing around and confess already. "I suppose half a million would set me up for life."

Darrell snorted. "Yeah. I'll cut you a check."

"Like you cut Melanie?"

"A conscience can be fatal in this business. I hadn't planned on—" Darrell stopped himself.

"Killing her?" PC offered.

Darrell's chuckle was menacing rather than mirthful. "Yes. And Branislav knew it when he came to meet me. He cried like a baby. Such an undignified way to die. I hope you won't do that." He scooped up the package and stood up. "Watch your back. Miss PC."

She watched him stride toward the exit, only to be met by half a dozen Possumwood PD officers and a Mirabella County sheriff's deputy. He faced her as they cuffed and disarmed him.

The detective smiled and tapped the unassuming pendant she wore. His shoulders slumped and his head dropped.

Chapter 16

DARLA, HOPE, AND Rocky sat on one side of the table. Terry, Rose, and PC sat on the other. The detective looked at the empty chair at the end of the table and wondered if she should have invited Drew. She was aware of how much he liked *Truffles!*, especially their wine list.

"I'm gonna miss y'all so much." Rocky put his arm around Hope's shoulders.

Rose unwrapped her silverware. "You gonna stay in Dallas, honey?"

"I think so. I was worried about it, because Justin would be there, but apparently he got fired already. Cecelia—one of my bridesmaids—heard it from his sister."

"It'll be good to have you closer." Rocky beamed.

Darla sliced open the roll on her bread plate. "We'll have a fun week setting up your new apartment." She smiled, but it didn't reach her eyes.

Hope put her head on Darla's shoulder for a moment. "Oh, Mom. I know you want me to come back to Seattle with you, but I really need to try something different."

Darla gave her daughter a sad smile.

PC would miss her niece when she and Darla left in the morning. But now, it was time for a family dinner. She sat back and listened to Rocky recount the tale of Meadowlark Moving.

Rocky plopped himself down on the couch and reached for the remote. Rose stepped into her bedroom. PC sat next to her brother, and Cordite jumped onto the couch between them, clearly hoping for double the petting.

"So, Rock? Do you really think Hope's going to be okay on her own?"

"Why do you ask?"

"That medication she's on. Looks like she's… got some issues."

Rocky clicked on the TV. "Well, that's where you're wrong."

"Oh?"

"Yup." He started clicking through the channels. "When her stepdad stepped out on her and Darla, Hope took it personal. She was just a kid, and kids are like that. She…" He looked down at his outstretched legs. "She quit eatin'. Almost had to go in the hospital. That medicine she's on? It's for her anorexia. It's what they call an 'off label' prescription, but it's the only thing that helped her. She don't take it all the time, just when she's feelin' stressed."

PC smiled at her brother and patted him on the knee. "Good to know, Rock. I'm beat. See you in the morning."

Another Thursday, another dive into the cold cases. The box of old photos smelled of dust and despair. Crime scene photos from thirty years ago. Photography equipment might have changed over the years, but murder hadn't. She sighed. There was a good chance the killer was already dead, or, with any luck, rotting away in prison for another crime.

Tran knocked on the door. "Hey, PC. Just wanted to tell you. Based on the information from Devyani, Kalindi, and Anu, Customs intercepted a modified container at the port. Five kids. The youngest one was ten."

PC sighed. "Now that they've learned to spot them, the bad guys'll change it up. Just another game of whack-a-mole. But I'm glad those kids were saved."

"Well, Cvetka cut a deal and flipped on Jagoda. She laid out the whole operation. They started out with moving stolen paintings by stretching an amateur canvas over the actual painting and keeping it secured with a sturdy frame. There aren't a huge number of stolen paintings, so they quickly moved on to forgeries. They used the same technique to ship them. Then someone in their network would claim to have found it in their grandma's attic or something. They were worth less money without provenance, but there was an art dealer who authenticated for them, for a fee."

"There always is. What about Leidecker?"

"Which one? There were three of them."

PC raised her eyebrows.

"But *our* Darrell Leidecker's real name is Adam Firestone. Lot of jurisdictions have been looking for him. Pretty much you name it, he's done it. That package you picked up? Counterfeit bills. He won't see the outside of a cell for the rest of his life."

A gurgle from PC's stomach told her it was nearly lunchtime. "I'm glad the Golobs got caught, but I feel bad for the businesses that regularly used that venue."

"Don't. The feds seized the property and it'll get turned over to the county. They're already discussing how to turn the place into a community center."

When PC got home from her fruitless cold case review, she found a large manilla envelope addressed to her on the kitchen table. Her tenant, Felicity, had sent her mail.

Bank statement.

Letter from a realty company wanting to buy her house.

Advertisement for a retirement planning seminar at a fancy steakhouse.

Something from Harris County.

PC folded the perforated edges and pulled them off, then opened the notice.

"Great. A jury summons."

She sighed. At least she could look forward to dinner with Drew tomorrow. Fresh new restaurant should be fun.

Hopefully, no one would turn up dead this time.

If you enjoyed this book, please consider leaving a review at your favorite book site. Reviews help other readers find and enjoy new books!

Other books by Holly Dey:

Manor of Death: The Possumwood Mysteries Book 1

Death on the Half Shell: The Possumwood Mysteries Book 2

Azalea Trail of Death: The Possumwood Mysteries Book 3

Death Re-Enacted: The Possumwood Mysteries Book 4

Death Rides a Bobcat: The Possumwood Mysteries Book 5

Key to Death: The Possumwood Mysteries Book 6

Death Curated: The Possumwood Mysteries Book 7

Pool of Death: The Possumwood Mysteries Book 8

All Death No Cattle: The Possumwood Mysteries Book 9

Death is Lager than Life: The Possumwood Mysteries Book 10

Art of Death: The Possumwood Mysteries Book 11

Little Town of Death-Lehem: The Possumwood Mysteries Book 12

Winter: Boxset Collection Books 1-3

Spring: Boxset Collection Books 4-6

Summer: Boxset Collection Books 7-9

Fall: Boxset Collection Books 10-12

All of the Possumwood Mysteries are available in

Large Print Editions